I0818191

Tales

From the

Cityverse:

A Short Story Collection

Tales From the Cityverse:

A Short Story Collection

Zoe van Lingen

This is a work of fiction. Names, characters, places, and incidents either are the product of the author's imagination or are used fictitiously. Any resemblance to actual persons, living or dead, events, or locales is entirely coincidental.

Cover design by Lena Yang

ISBN: 978-1-7383568-0-5

Also by Zoe van Lingen

The Liberator Duology

The Liberator

The Vanquisher

Causes and Courtships

To my grandma Joanne

1932-2023

Rebuilding From Loss

Vera

Vera woke with a start to her mom's screams. Weeks prior, her dad had booked himself an appointment at the Clinic for his illness that had lingered for weeks and gotten progressively worse. Vera had never known anyone to do that and had only gone on Clinic Day when the Government mandated it. At first, the medicine the Clinic prescribed her dad had helped. Lately, he'd been weak, tired and pale, and his appetite was gone. She feared the worst with her mom's screams and leapt out of bed.

Her mom's screams turned to sobbing, and Vera hesitated outside her parents' door. Did she really want to see this? If she went back to bed and tuned out the noise, she could convince herself it had been a nightmare. *No.* She wasn't a little girl anymore. Whatever had happened, she could face it.

Vera inhaled a deep breath, opened the door and stepped into her parents' dark bedroom. "Mom? What's wrong? I heard screaming."

Vera waited for her mom to say it was nothing, just a nightmare and to go back to bed. Her mom didn't do that. She sniffled and let the tears stream down her face. "Summon a guard, Vera."

Her mom sounded weary, in a way that spoke of more than loss of sleep. She bent over her husband, letting sobs wrack her body.

Vera fled the room. Her dad hadn't moved, nor had he said anything. Perhaps the worst had come, but Vera refused to think of that now. She pulled on a pair of shoes, grabbed her ID pass and a key, and left her apartment. The only ways to summon a guard were to use the apartment manager's phone or find a guard on the street. As it was the middle of the night, Vera went with the second option. When she reached the lobby of her building, her heart raced, and her palms sweated. Going outside at night had always been forbidden, except for on the fire escape platform. This could end with her in prison, yet what choice did she have? She had to help her parents.

She placed her hand on the door and couldn't make herself move. Her legs shook, and she toppled over. How was she going to do this? Tears pooled in her eyes, both from the scene in her parents' room and her own helplessness.

In the misty patch of vision through the door, a light flickered. Vera wiped away tears to get a better look. Perhaps it had been a faulty streetlight or a trick of her mind. *No*. It was a flashlight. There was a guard on patrol walking past her door.

This was her one chance. Vera pushed herself upright, opened the door and called out. "Please! I need help."

The guard stopped in his tracks and turned around, pointing his flashlight at Vera. Her feet were still within the building, so he couldn't arrest her for that. She wasn't technically outside.

Vera gulped as the guard kept his flashlight on her. He was like a robot, or a statue, impossible to read. "Please. Something's happened to my dad."

The guard held out his scanner. "Show me your ID pass."

Vera held it up with a steady hand, and the scanner beeped upon reading it. That had to be a good sign, right?

The guard nodded. "Take me to your apartment."

Vera opened the door wider to let the guard in, and she called the elevator. It came quick at that hour and zoomed upward to her floor. The guard trailed her to her apartment, and she directed him to her parents' bedroom where her mom still sat hunched over her husband's body and crying.

The guard pulled a device out of one of his pockets, tapped its flat surface and brought it to the side of his face. He waited a moment then spoke into it. Vera made out the words: 'ambulance', 'clinic' and 'emergency'. He wasn't speaking loudly enough for her to hear entire sentences.

He went over to Vera's mom, who nodded and sat up, freeing her husband's body for the guard to see. Guards had no medical training, so there was nothing he could do for Vera's dad.

Vera waited by the bedroom doorway. If she stayed still and out of the way, no one would make her leave. Something was seriously wrong for her dad not to have moved or made a noise, but Vera didn't want to think the worst.

She had to answer the door when the Clinic staff came. They were one of the few professions, if not the only one outside of guards, that could get an exception to the curfew. Two had come, dressed in white coats and carrying a stretcher between them.

They both looked tired and bleary eyed from being called into action at such a late hour, but one flashed Vera a small and kind smile. "Where is your dad?"

"In the bedroom," Vera said, turning on her heel and waving them after her. "This way."

When the Clinic staff reached the bedroom, the guard exited and pulled out his talking device again. Vera left him to speak to whomever it connected to and snuck into the bedroom.

Her mom was sobbing as the Clinic staff examined her dad with tools and equipment from the bags on their backs. Vera heard her dad moan as they lifted him onto the stretcher and secured his body. The sound gave Vera hope. He wasn't gone yet.

The kind one pulled out a piece of paper and a pen and scribbled out a note for Vera's mom. "You can visit at this address in the morning. We'll do all we can."

Vera's mom took the note with a shaky hand and dipped her head, seeming unable to form words.

The Clinic staff lifted the stretcher and walked out of the bedroom.

"Wait!" Vera called as she rushed over to the stretcher to grab her dad's hand. It felt cold, and he made no effort to squeeze back. From up close, she could see him breathing in shallow pants, and that his skin had lost all its colour. Her dad had always looked like her, with brown skin and eyes, and dark hair; he was a muted version now. "Is he going to be okay?"

The kind one met Vera's eyes. "We won't know until we run tests and find out what's wrong. You can see him in the morning,"

There was no amount of begging that would convince them to let her go with her dad. Vera didn't even try. She swallowed the lump in her throat, let the Clinic staff leave, walked to her mom and sat on the bed beside her. "What happened?"

Her mom sniffed and swiped at her eyes. When she spoke, her voice warbled. "I felt the bed shake. He had convulsions, and then just went still and quiet."

Vera understood little in terms of medicine and illnesses. Most people couldn't afford to treat anything serious. Her parents were lucky. Paying for her dad's medicine hadn't bankrupted them yet, though they had cut expenses where they could. Vera hoped her dad would get better. They needed his income. "I'm going back to bed," she announced, which earned her a slight nod and nothing more from her mom.

Vera knew, as she went into her own bedroom, that her mom wasn't going to sleep. She likely wouldn't either, but the quiet and calm of her room would at least help her process.

In the morning, Vera rubbed her groggy eyes and went into the kitchenette to fetch breakfast. Her mom was still in her room, seeming unmotivated to move. With a sigh, Vera added a second bread slice to the toaster and, when it popped, took a slice to her mom.

Her mom shoved it away. "I'm not hungry."

Vera pushed it back, feeling like the parent for once. It was odd, but someone needed to take be strong and take control. "You need to eat. It won't do anyone any good if you don't have your strength when we go see dad."

Her mom took a bite of toast, her eyes unfocused and distant. It was like she'd already given up.

Vera still had hope, however foolish it was. The only way she could keep going was to cling to that hope. She plucked the Clinic staff's note from her parents' bedside table and settled her eyes on her mom. "When you're done eating, make yourself presentable. I'll figure out which bus we need."

Once Vera was fed and dressed, she went downstairs to check the bus map against the address the Clinic staff had left. It was different from the outpatient Clinic Vera went to on Clinic Day and the one her dad had gone to for medicine. Because her parents were paying, her dad wasn't at the End Camp. Instead, he was in the City's hospital where the ultra rich went to treat serious illnesses.

Vera ran her finger along the listed routes. There wasn't one that went completely from her apartment to the hospital. They'd need to make two connections, and Vera tried to commit them to memory, moving her lips as she recited the listed bus numbers in her mind.

With her mom in such a fragile state, it was up to Vera to be the calm and responsible one. She would emulate her dad, as that was the role he played in their family. Perhaps seeing Vera remain calm would give him strength.

When she was confident in memorizing the bus route, Vera returned to her apartment to usher her mom downstairs. When they got on the first bus, her mom clung to her hand. Her eyes were misty, and her shoulders had a hunch. "I don't know what to do, Vera. How will we cope?"

Vera patted her mom on the arm, like she was soothing a child. "Dad will be fine. He'll recover, go back to work and we'll manage." She said it as much for her own sake as her mom's. The alternative was too difficult to think about.

Vera had to give the City credit for keeping its buses on an efficient schedule. She and her mom made the transfer without having to wait long in between, and before she knew whether she was ready, they were walking the path to the hospital door.

It wasn't an intimidating building. From the outside, it could've been any high rise. The interior was all white, like most City buildings run by the Government. As Vera and her mom stepped in the door, an orderly ushered them to the registration desk where her mom gave the nurse Vera's dad's name.

The nurse tapped a screen built into her desk. From Vera's angle, all she could see was glare. She wasn't mean to read it or decipher it like the nurse was.

When the nurse found what she was looking for, she glanced up at Vera and her mom. "Seventh floor, ward five. You can take the elevators down here," she pointed her pen over her shoulder and to the left. "Visiting time ends in four hours."

Vera took her mom by the arm and led her to the elevator. Her mom still had blank eyes and slouched shoulders, which would do nothing to help her dad. Vera had always thought of her mom as formidable and brave, not empty and broken. What would she be like if the worst came? Vera wanted never to find out.

Her dad was prostrate on a cot with a curtain pulled most of the way around. Vera heard beeping and whirring of machines as she approached, and when she got close, she saw tubes and wires running from the machines to her dad. The setup, his hospital gown and pale face made him look like a stranger, not like the charismatic and strong man that had taught Vera how to bake and tie her shoes. It caused a knot of dread to form in her stomach, which she shoved her attention away from.

Her mom collapsed onto a chair situated beside his bed, but Vera went to him and took his hand. "Mom and I are here, Dad." It got no response. He just stayed still and quiet except for a wheeze as he breathed.

The machines and her mom's crying were louder than the wheeze, but the wheeze told Vera her dad was still hanging on. She clung to her dad's hand for a while, and eventually took to the other chair to watch her dad from the short distance.

"What are we going to do?" her mom wailed.

Vera closed her eyes and inhaled deep through her nose, willing the tension in her body to ease. "We're going to wait and hope."

The allotted visiting time dragged on with the sound of her mom's crying and muffled voices of people comforting other patients in the ward, each shrouded behind bed curtains. There was a comfort from knowing other people were in the same situation with a loved one in the hospital, but Vera had never felt so alone.

A nurse came to the ward and handed a piece of paper to Vera's mom before going to the next bed to do the same. Vera got a glance at it to see a summary of her dad's condition listed as critical, with a line saying he'd never woken up.

Her mom hardly glanced at the paper and shoved it away. "I can't go on without him."

Vera refused to think her dad wouldn't recover, which her mom had seemed to accept as an inevitability. How could her mom give up like that? "He's going to be fine."

That only made her mom cry harder, and she didn't stop through the rest of the visiting period, their bus rides home, or once she got back to her room.

It was up to Vera to cook and bring a plate to her mom. She thought her new responsibilities would be temporary, but as the days went by and her dad didn't get better, Vera went numb from trying to keep her mom from spiralling into a pit of despair. The only positives were that the rising medical bill had been enough to coax her mom into going to work, and Vera still had school to attend.

Her new routine and role reversal left Vera exhausted, so much so that she didn't see the official Government letter on the floor a week after her dad had gone to the hospital. He hadn't improved, had even developed a stronger wheeze, but with every visit fit in before classes, Vera had clung to her hope.

She tripped on the letter on her way out the door. If it hadn't had official Government insignia on it, she would've left it aside until she got home from school. It was the insignia that made her pick it up and open the seal.

Vera had thought numb was the worst she could feel. The pain that cascaded through her and broke her heart into millions of pieces as she read the letter announcing her dad's death was much worse.

Her mom screamed and doubled over when Vera brought the letter to her with a shaking hand. Perhaps a mom with more emotional strength would've tried to comfort her daughter, but Vera's mom retreated into herself and shooed Vera into the hallway. A closed door and the sound of wailing was all Vera got.

Vera brushed tears from her eyes, which was a futile gesture as new ones replaced them as she wiped. Sitting around her apartment was too dreadful and suffocating of an idea to entertain, and Vera couldn't go to school and pretend things were fine. She would explain the next day and let them add an absence to her record.

She needed one day to grieve with someone who would support her. At least she could have that much before restructuring her life.

Vera didn't bother to tell her mom where she was going, knowing she would get little in response. She grabbed her bag and her ID pass, pulled on a pair of boots and ran to the bus that would carry her to her friend Caleb's Apartment District.

Vera had met Caleb through volunteering to pack crates for Arlo Fenn's Cause when she was fourteen and he was sixteen. At eighteen, he was now old enough to work instead of going to school. Vera knew he'd be home in the morning, as his job was a bartender in a Restaurant Doma in Apartment District 1. The wealthy didn't go out for drinks in the morning. Restaurant Doma didn't open until noon, and their bar opened later than that.

Caleb blinked away his fatigue and ran a hand over his disheveled hair when he opened his apartment door and saw Vera. "It's early, V. Don't you have school?"

Vera bit down on her bottom lip and swiped away some tears to stem the stream of them on her face. "I can't." She took a deep breath, closed her eyes and said the words she never wanted to. "My dad died overnight."

Her words snapped Caleb awake, and his eyes bugged out before going soft, and he wrapped her into a hug. "I'm sorry, V."

Vera sagged in his arms and cried on his shoulder. If she had romantic interest in anyone, she liked to think it would've been Caleb. She'd never felt those feelings for anyone, hadn't had crushes or fantasies about kissing boys or doing more. Friendship had always been enough, and Caleb had accepted that without question.

Caleb stroked her back and ushered her into his apartment, sat her down on his couch and tucked a blanket around her. "I'll make tea, and you can say whatever you need to process."

Vera tucked her feet underneath her and nodded as he walked into his kitchenette. She felt safe at Caleb's. It wasn't that home felt unsafe, just tense and isolating, especially with her mom doing nothing except crying.

"I don't know what to do," she told Caleb when he came back with a mug of tea and a piece of toast. "I thought he'd get better, and he didn't."

Caleb perched on the couch beside Vera and rested his hand on her shoulder. "I know it's hard, even more so because you were close to him."

Vera drank a gulp of tea, letting it warm her from the inside. It was a small comfort, more than she was getting from her mom. "He looked so pale in the hospital that I almost didn't recognize him."

Caleb squeezed Vera's shoulder. "It'll hurt less with time. I promise."

Vera trusted Caleb, but that felt impossible at that moment. She couldn't imagine the pain of loss ever lessening. "I can't stand going home. My mom shut herself in her bedroom and won't speak to me."

"She's hurting too. You have to go home at some point. Making her worry about you won't help."

Vera drunk another large gulp of tea and dunked the toast in it before taking a bite. She was sure her mom hadn't noticed her leave. "I don't know what'll happen to us without dad's income or whether I can get my mom to go to work." She wanted her dad back more than anything, not just because of her now precarious financial situation. Talking about superficial things like money was easier than delving headfirst into her grief. It was a problem Caleb could help her solve, and he could do nothing to bring her dad back.

Caleb wrapped his arms around Vera. "You both need time to grieve. No one expects you to move on like nothing happened. When you're ready, I can call in a favour and get you a job with me. That'll take some pressure off your mom."

Vera leaned into Caleb's side and looked up at him. "You think I'm ready for a job?" She'd hoped to finish high school and even attend the university. However, with the large medical bill to pay off, the university was likely out of reach. Still, Vera couldn't quit school, not without a Courtship, and she would never have one of those.

"At least on the weekends. Mr. Polman's looking for a new dishwasher. Our current one just gave their notice."

Dish washing was something Vera knew how to do, though she couldn't imagine spending all day doing that to go home and wash more dishes. "I don't know, Caleb."

Caleb donned a cheeky grin. "Comes with a free meal per shift and a share of the tips. The base pay's pretty high. You might be able to save up for university tuition."

Vera did like the idea of bringing in her own money, and spending weekends in her apartment with her mom shut in her bedroom was a less appealing option. "I'll think about it and talk to my mom. She might have an opinion."

"Of course, V. Take whatever time you need."

Vera finished her mug of tea and slice of toast, then helped Caleb clean up. She needed to feel busy and useful to get her mind off the absence of her dad. Her apartment would never be the same with the hole he left behind. Perhaps Caleb was right that working would be good for her.

When she got home, Vera's tears were dried up, and she held her chin high as she went to her mom's door and knocked. "Mom? We need to talk."

Her mom mumbled something Vera couldn't hear through the door, so she opened the door and walked in. Her mom still lay on the bed, her face buried in her arms, though she wasn't actively sobbing.

"I miss him too," Vera said. "But you have to talk to me. Please don't shut me out."

Her mom lifted her head and turned it in Vera's direction with dull, tired eyes. "We've lost everything. I don't know how to go on, only that I must."

Vera pursed her lips. Wasn't she a good enough reason for her mom to try? "We both must, and we can do it together."

Her mom lowered her head, no longer looking at Vera. "I need to be alone."

Vera left her mom's room. She assumed, in time, that her mom would come out and speak to her. They could help each other grieve. Yet, her mom turned inward. She left the apartment for work, as she had to help pay down the medical bill Vera's dad's income had been covering. When her mom was home, she shut herself in her bedroom, transforming it into a shrine to her dead husband.

The daily chores and errands fell on Vera. After a week, when she prepared to go grocery shopping and the budget was a quarter of what it had once been, Vera knew she had to do something.

She returned to her mom's room, now stuffed with her dad's belongings and pictures of him, leaving only a side of the bed uncovered where her mom perched day and night when she wasn't at work.

Her mom didn't bother to lift her head and look at Vera. "I left the grocery money on the table."

"I know." It was in Vera's pocket. "It's not enough."

Her mom heaved a sigh. "It has to be. We need to cut expenses where we can."

Vera knew this from the amount listed as due on the letter the hospital had sent announcing her dad's death. Her mom's salary wasn't enough. "Caleb said I could get a job with him. I'm going to take him up on it."

Her announcement got barely a nod from her mom. Vera knew things would never return to what they'd been. Her childhood was effectively over, and it was up to her now to manage the bills and run the apartment. Her mom had given up, living only for the purpose of paying a medical debt for the man she loved.

Vera went into the living room and wrote out a note for Caleb she would post on her way to the market. No longer could she put it off. She would take the job, if only to save up so she could move out at eighteen and start a life on her own. Sitting idly by while her mom descended further into inconsolable grief each day would stifle her. A part of Vera had died alongside her dad, but she would build herself up from the remnants.

Starting a New Life

Kelsie

Kelsie woke to a knock on the door of the storage room she slept in. She rolled off the pile of rags that served as her makeshift bed, got to her feet and crossed the small area of bare floor. All in all, it wasn't the worst room she'd slept in during her years with Arlo Fenn. At least it had solid walls, and the roof didn't leak.

Arlo Fenn was on the other side of the door, fist raised to knock again. He lowered it and jammed it into his pocket when Kelsie opened the door. "Get ready. I've got a new job for you."

Kelsie nodded and retreated into the room to retrieve some clean clothes from her bag of belongings. She owned very little, all of which Arlo had given her. He wasn't her father, though he'd been the one to take her from the Foster Centre. He'd made it clear from the first day that he was her guardian, and she would work for her keep. Ever since, Kelsie had helped him move black market goods around the City and sometimes to the Colony. In between, Arlo bounced her from abandoned building to abandoned building, giving her a series of forged ID passes. Without a permanent address, she couldn't have a real ID pass. It was an unpredictable life with little stability, yet still magnitudes better than living in the Foster Centre.

Kelsie threw on her clean clothes, finger combed her hair, wiped the sleep crust from her eyes and laced her boots. After a deep breath and some stretches to work out the kinks in her muscles she'd gained overnight, she went to join Arlo Fenn.

"Where's the job this time?" she asked as she followed him down the hallway to the room he'd commandeered as a kitchenette and pantry. She was alone in this place most of the time, having proved to Arlo over the years that she wasn't going to run away. There was nowhere to go. Kelsie was an orphan who had no friends or family to stay with, and trying to survive on the streets was impossible with the guard patrols. She might've risked it if it weren't for stories of prisoners never coming home.

Arlo plucked a can of fruit cocktail off a shelf, pulled the tab on its lid and poured the contents into a bowl, which he handed to Kelsie with a spoon. "Got a request from the Colony. We're picking up supplies to store here until the runners come to deliver them."

Kelsie took the bowl of fruit and maneuvered her spoon to get a bite. She usually got her own meals, but Arlo must've been in a hurry today or feeling generous. As she ate, he filled water flasks and packed dried fruit and nuts into a bag. Kelsie shook her head behind his back. If there was a moment, she would add some actual food. She couldn't survive on fruits and nuts if she was going to be out working all day.

"You're using new runners?" He would've mentioned names if he was using ones she'd met and worked with before.

Arlo tucked the flasks into the bag and zipped it. He didn't turn to look at her. "They're only new to Colony runs, and you're going with them. I need your experience to ensure things go as planned."

Kelsie liked her previous trips to the Colony. It was a refreshing change of pace to leave the Wall. Staying within the confines of the City was stifling, especially since she had no real home in it or place to plant roots. "You won't be disappointed."

When Arlo finished with his bag, he strode towards the door. "Wash that bowl out when you're finished. We need to get going."

Kelsie didn't get to see the side of Arlo he reserved for people he recruited into the Cause. She only got the gruff and direct version, though she'd caught glimpses of his passion when they were out on jobs together. She finished her fruit, rinsed her bowl and grabbed some granola bars and crackers to shove in her pockets. There was no time for sandwich making.

Alro was waiting for her by the main entrance, and he went outside when he saw her coming. Kelsie was only a few steps behind him and clambered onto the passenger seat of his truck, fastening her seatbelt as he pulled away.

He drove to a run-down warehouse on the edge of Apartment District 11, likely on the Government's list of buildings needing replacement based on its crumbling appearance. The Cause often took temporary possession of such places to store and distribute goods.

What was different about this trip, from prior ones Kelsie had taken, was bringing the crates and sacks back to where she was staying. Usually, Arlo would drive to a drop off point for local runners to distribute on their own.

"Why are we storing it?" Kelsie asked on the drive back to her temporary home. Her arms ached from hefting the sacks and crates and single duffle bag of medicine onto the bed of Arlo's truck, and she'd only have to move them again when they returned. Her stomach growled. She was still hungry after eating Arlo's packed snacks and her own in the hours it had taken to get into the warehouse and retrieve everything.

Arlo kept his eyes on the road, not sparing her a glance. "The runners lost their local building. It wasn't Cause property, so there was nothing I could do except offer them a Colony run."

Kelsie knew better than to ask for details on the runners or how they'd lost their building. Arlo wouldn't tell her. She wasn't supposed to get attached to anyone, lest she think about running off. Kelsie yearned for a place she could call home. Somewhere she knew she'd go every night to lay her head on a real bed, and cook and eat in a real kitchen, with a genuine ID pass in her pocket. Of course, she was grateful to Arlo for taking her in, but he wasn't family or even her friend. She wanted someone who cared about her as a person, not just as a resource or employee they could exploit. Maybe this time she'd stay in the Colony and integrate herself in the community of exiles there. Arlo wouldn't waste effort on fetching her.

She bit back her groans as she helped Arlo move the cargo into her already crowded room, leaving only a narrow strip of bare floor. When they were finished, she flopped onto her makeshift bed, stretching her arms out to her sides.

Arlo lingered in her doorway, one hand on the knob. "While you're gone, I'm going to clear this place out. It's time to move on."

Kelsie pressed her lips into a firm line as she pushed herself up to sitting. Moving on meant she had to bring her belongings with her and destroy evidence of having been in the abandoned building before she left it. Arlo never cleaned out her room. It was always her responsibility. She gathered up her dirty clothes to wash in the shower with dish soap and hang them to dry on the shower rod. With no more than a few outfits, there was plenty of room, and they would dry quickly with the heat of the building. Arlo had rigged the water and lights on when he moved Kelsie into the place, though he hadn't activated the cooling system.

Kelsie wiped the sweat from her brow and went to the pantry to scrounge together a meal of canned beans and rice. She'd survived for as long as she could remember on whatever foods Arlo could get for cheap. Feeding her wasn't a food law violation as Arlo used permits granting him permission to buy on her behalf, similar to what scientists south of the Outskirts used to order their supplies. That didn't mean he bought her high-end foods. It would've been nice to have a proper meal for once, but she wasn't sure her taste buds could handle it. Almost everything she ate was either salty from being canned or bland.

While her meal cooked, she made some peanut butter sandwiches and snacks for the journey to the Colony and back. If she stayed in the Colony, at least she would have a couple meals to tide her over.

She ate her meal in the pantry, leaning against the counter the hotplate sat atop. Arlo hadn't provided furniture since she'd been small and lived with him. Once she'd turned eleven, that had stopped, and she'd cried herself to sleep for days. At least back then he'd come every morning to take her to school and had driven her back every afternoon. These days, she did her learning wherever she lived, using textbooks and pamphlets Arlo brought her. It wasn't the same as going to school, but no one cared whether she attended high school or not anyway.

With her stomach full, Kelsie retrieved her clothes from the shower rod and packed her bag. All her belongings, plus two days' worth of food, fit in one bag. All she needed to add was a checkpoint pass, which Arlo would supply before she left.

She spent most of the night lying awake, wondering where Arlo would send her next. Wherever it was, she didn't want to go. It wasn't that she'd miss this place, but she was tired of bouncing around to avoid Government detection. This could be an opportunity to eek out a life for herself where she got to make decisions and had some stability.

In the morning, Kelsie saw that Arlo had slid a Checkpoint pass under the door. She crouched to pick it up and put it in her bag on the top. All there was left to do was wait.

To pass the time, she made herself a breakfast of porridge. It would've tasted better had Arlo stocked the pantry with cinnamon or sugar, except he didn't spend money on spices for her. Still, she swallowed the porridge to fill her stomach. Her next meal would likely be on the road, eaten amongst strangers. Perhaps they would judge her food, or her as a person. It didn't matter.

Kelsie had traveled with groups of Cause supporters before. She never made friends or lasting contact with any of them. Arlo had warned her when she was small not to get too close to anyone. That would only make it more difficult for her to move on when she needed to, and it would just add suspicion onto her. To protect herself, she couldn't form relationships.

It was lonely, and Kelsie often craved contact with another person. She settled for Arlo's visits, which weren't enough. If she'd been a normal girl going to high school and on dates, she might've been thinking of a Courtship this year, since she was sixteen. As it was, she knew no one her age to apply for one with.

Arlo had never gotten a Courtship, choosing to devout his life to the Cause and helping the least fortunate. He didn't understand Kelsie's urge for affection, so she didn't broach the subject, opting to bottle up her emotions around him. He would only be hurt and disappointed to learn she wanted to leave the kind of life she had in search of something better. Why should she mention that when it was never a possibility?

When Kelsie finished her porridge and washed the bowl and spoon, she went back to her room. It was a better choice than sitting by the front door waiting for Arlo or the runners to arrive. That would only make her appear desperate and impatient.

She wiled the time away neatening up the stack of fabrics she'd need to burn and finding a lighter. With the lighter collected, she flopped on the makeshift bed, deciding that was preferable to standing like a pathetic statue.

With no clock in the room, Kelsie didn't know how much time had passed when two knocks sounded on her door followed by Arlo inquiring as to whether she was inside. She got to her feet, biting back her groan, and cracked open the door to respond, choosing to be sarcastic. She nodded when he asked if the cargo was ready. This wasn't her first time going on a supply run, and she'd thought he'd trust her to have the basics down by now.

Kelsie opened her door, revealing three teenagers – a girl and two boys – standing behind Arlo. She made the quick decision to delegate moving the crates to the boys and enlisting the girl in helping burn her bedding in one of the vacant cement rooms Arlo always insisted Kelsie's living quarters had. She dumped the fabric on the burn marks of the windowless room's floor and instructed the girl to light them.

As Kelsie returned to her, now former, room to retrieve the rest of the fabrics, she thought about what she was getting herself into. These were teenagers she was about to ride to the Colony with. It was likely their first time south of the Wall, which brought risks. Normally, the Colony runners were older and more experienced, not newbies acting scared as if a Guard had caught them outside after curfew. She only hoped the girl wasn't going to be the driver as she looked out of her element.

When the fabrics were on fire, Kelsie took the girl back to her room to fetch her backpack; the sacks and the duffle bag of medicine Kelsie kept close to her body. This was going to be a stressful trip, and she would need to keep a high alert. Normally, Kelsie had trust in Arlo, but perhaps he sensed that she wanted to leave and decided he'd rather set her up to be arrested than let her go.

If the worst came, Kelsie would run. It didn't matter where. She didn't owe these people anything, didn't even know their names, which she was quick to rectify. Jack and Ethan were the boys who'd carried the crates, and Amelia was the girl.

Arlo disappeared while Kelsie had burned the fabrics. It was just like him to not say goodbye. He just assumed she'd be back. She would show him. Her time living where he put her was over, one way or another.

There were more people involved in this supply run: a boy named Malcolm and a girl named Dina. Kelsie was an interlope trapped in their friend group. There was no going back though, and the Colony needed supplies, so Kelsie gave some sass and strode to the side of their van with her head high. It was interesting to note there was tension between Malcolm and Jack Maybe they weren't all united against her.

Her seat ended up beside Ethan, who was the only one of the group that didn't seem to be part of a couple. He gave her a small, friendly smile as she settled in with her backpack and the duffle bag. Perhaps the drive wouldn't be so terrible. At least the seat was comfortable, and she had leg room without her knees being squished into the back of the seat ahead of her. She'd ridden in worse vehicles with scarier people.

Kelsie had wondered why Arlo hadn't given her a Gate pass until she met Malcolm, their driver who had eyes only for Amelia. He was the one least like the others, considering the fancy clothes he was wearing and that he had access to a van. Both facts screamed to Kelsie that he had money the rest of the group didn't. Why was he here? Was it to impress Amelia? Or was it to soothe his own ego and conscience?

It wasn't a topic she puzzled for long as she had to provide directions, pointed through the windshield, once they were south of the Wall. Soon, it became clear that the group had no experience south of the City and were unaware of the checkpoint. She blamed Arlo for this. He'd granted them this delivery without preparing them for all its aspects. Perhaps Arlo had just assumed she'd handle it, and she would because she had to, but she was finished doing little tasks for him that could've been avoided.

Kelsie's stomach always twisted into knots when she had to present her ID pass. It was a sophisticated fake designed not to set off the scanners, yet there was still a chance that she'd get caught. At least she'd perfected how to appear calm, and keep her hand steady, when she handed up ID passes and the checkpoint pass fetched from her bag.

Kelsie bristled when Malcolm revealed he had his own checkpoint pass, though she couldn't blame him for testing her. He was smart not to blindly trust her, and she started to think Arlo had only sent her to chaperone the medicine duffle bag and to give Malcolm directions. Perhaps Arlo thought having her there would ensure the cargo would get to the Colony, but he'd never have any proof of it reaching its destination other than oral testimony from the runners and Kelsie.

It was Jack, sitting In the back beside his girlfriend Dina, whom Kelsie didn't trust, and she returned his barbs with her own. She didn't appreciate being accused of smuggling food, like she was reckless and had no qualms about breaking the food laws. Previous runners, who'd acted on their own, had tried and failed. They'd earned a one-way ticket to the prison for their attempt, never to be heard from again. Arlo always kept his deliveries within the confines of the laws, only smuggling unrestricted goods. Breaking the food laws wasn't worth the cost.

Once Jack ceased his accusations, there was little for Kelsie to do. She munched on some of her snacks as the others calmed down from their terror at facing a guard. On the way back it would be worse; it always was. Vehicles driving north got more scrutiny from the Government out of suspicion and fear over people returning from the Colony. They had few qualms about letting people flee to the Colony, never to return. It was those who returned from the Colony that worried the Government and led to arrest warrants. Kelsie wondered what excuse Malcolm would provide on the return trip. There were few plausible and legitimate reasons to be south of the Outskirts and come back, checkpoint pass or not.

As Malcolm drove on and the hours passed, Amelia drifted to sleep, as did Dina and Jack. It was a very long drive, and Kelsie forced herself to stay awake. She was too tense around strangers to let herself relax that much, especially in a closed space traveling through the middle of nowhere.

What Kelsie didn't expect was for Ethan to stay awake too. She thought it would only be her and Malcolm, but Ethan had his sparkling brown eyes on her. He had his arms crossed loosely in his lap and his back reclined against the seat, looking the picture of someone at ease.

He was handsome with his brown hair, not that different from hers in colour, and his angled cheekbones. Her heartbeat quickened when she glanced at him and saw him smile. She had no reason to react that way to a boy, let alone one she hardly knew.

"I'm sorry you had to bring me along," Kelsie told Malcolm, deciding that looking at the back of his headrest was better than out the window or at Ethan. "You could've managed this without me."

"Don't apologize," Malcolm said. "Your experience is valuable."

Kelsie shook her head. "I'm only as valuable as Arlo believes I am. Most of the time, it doesn't feel like much."

"Tying your self worth to him must feel terrible," Ethan said.

Kelsie's body went rigid. No one usually noticed her, let alone made observations. The truth was, Kelsie knew she was only worth as much as Arlo thought. There was no one who cared about her, and her life was what Arlo made it. "I don't know what it feels like not to."

Ethan looked at her with a frown. "I'm sorry. I don't envy you living under Arlo's control."

Kelsie hardly knew Ethan, but he peered beneath the barriers she kept around herself and saw her at her core. Her heart sped up its pace whenever she caught his eyes. It wasn't a reaction she had around anyone, and she didn't know what to make of it, other than she wanted to speak to him more. The van wasn't the place for that, not with Malcolm present. "Arlo's the closest person I have to family."

It obviously wasn't convincing as Ethan's frown deepened. "I understand what it's like to be an outsider no one cares about. I wouldn't wish it on anyone."

Kelsie wouldn't have believed those words from anyone else in the van. It was seeing Ethan on the edge of the larger group while the others were coupled up that made his statement credible. She'd assumed he had other friends, even a potential Courtship partner. Perhaps he didn't. Perhaps all his friends were in the van, and he was the odd person out. Was Kelsie so desperate for a connection to someone that she'd fall instantly for the first person who had something in common with her? She hoped not, even if it was a plausible explanation for her racing heart and the butterflies in her stomach.

The other explanation was that Ethan was just handsome and kind, and she was having an involuntary reaction. Something inside her, hidden behind the anxiety she locked away from prying eyes, was drawn to him, and it made her cheeks warm with a blush.

"You shouldn't worry about me. After tomorrow, we'll go back to our lives like this trip didn't happen." That was how things always went after a Colony supply run. The runners moved on, and Kelsie went back to Arlo. This time, she wouldn't go back to him, but Ethan and Malcolm didn't need to know that.

"Is that what you want?" Malcolm asked. "Or what Arlo told you to do?"

"I always do what he tells me." It was difficult to know what she wanted, though she knew it wasn't the life she had. Arlo wouldn't fulfil anything more than a minor food request anyway.

"What are you going to do when you've outlasted your usefulness?"

This time Malcolm met her gaze through the rearview mirror. He had inviting green eyes that held no judgement, but they did nothing to stir her emotions like Ethan's did. That was good, considering how much attention he paid Amelia.

Kelsie inhaled a shaky breath. It wasn't a hard question, and she knew the answer, though she'd never admitted it to anyone. "I'll take care of myself."

That only deepened Ethan's frown even further. If anyone else had looked at Kelsie the way he did, she would've felt pitied and fled. On him, the expression looked sympathetic and understanding, like he could relate to her experience. She didn't know whether he could or couldn't. Perhaps, once they got to the Colony, she could get him alone, and they could speak freely.

She occupied time with gazing out the window and nibbling on her food. When the others woke up and started discussing the Colony, Kelsie acted on an impulse she didn't know she had and flirted with Ethan. She enjoyed the blush on his cheeks she got for calling him hot. Her own cheeks started to hurt from the grin that blossomed on her face, which she morphed into a smirk with some effort. Letting Amelia or Ethan see her glee wasn't an option. She needed to remain detached. It was the only way she could make a clean break from Arlo.

To take her mind off Ethan, she turned her attention on Malcolm. It didn't make sense that he'd do all this just to impress Amelia, nor did she understand why he had his own checkpoint pass. She should've guessed his parents were involved. Some of the City's rich had interests south the City, and a select few helped the Colony out of charity or to get back at the Government for their restrictive food laws.

Malcolm was a puzzle Kelsie didn't endeavour to solve. He was Amelia's, not hers, and she didn't want him. She was also happy to leave Jack to Dina. It was Ethan she wanted to get alone.

That had to wait. When they arrived at the Colony, Kelsie helped unload and move the cargo, keeping the medicine duffle bag with her until it was time to place it in the storage shed. Her job was now complete. If she'd wanted to, she could've left the group and stayed put in the Colony. It had been her plan before Ethan and his dazzling eyes. Now, she fell into line with the group and memorized the house the Colonists left Ethan and Jack at.

At first, Kelsie walked alone behind the woman carrying the flashlight while Dina and Amelia bickered. When Amelia sped up to leave Dina behind, Kelsie took her chance on Amelia being the more approachable of the two to ask about Ethan. Before she went to speak with him, she had to be sure he didn't have someone waiting at home.

"I think he's been overlooked and ignored," Amelia said to Kelsie's remark. "No one, except Jack, really gives him any attention."

This fit with the picture Kelsie had formed of him from this short trip. It was certainly something she related to, as even Arlo barely paid Kelsie any attention. "Do you think he'd talk to me?"

"I don't know." Amelia said. "I have no experience with guys."

Kelsie wanted to roll her eyes. Perhaps it was true, but Amelia had Malcolm invested in her. Surely, she had to see that.

When the woman with the flashlight finally stopped at the house meant for Kelsie, Dina and Amelia, Kelsie claimed the room with the single bed. They couldn't expect her to share with someone she hardly knew, and she wasn't going to argue.

She closed the bedroom door, dropped her backpack, opened the window and climbed out. When her boots hit the ground, she ran, mentally counting the houses until she reached the one designated for Ethan and Jack.

Ethan was alone with his and Jack's bags. He smiled when he saw Kelsie, and she reached for his hand. She never would've risked that in the City, but affection laws didn't matter here. His hand was warm and fit with hers better than she would've imagined. Sparks travelled up her arm, and butterflies flew through her stomach.

Her eyes met his. He was tall, yet not so tall that she got a crick in her neck to gaze up at him. "I'd like to talk."

"Alright," he said. "Let's go outside in case Jack comes back."

Kelsie followed him outside and around to the back of the building. She felt like she was flying in the clouds, and her life with Arlo was worlds away as she and Ethan walked. The only person that mattered was Ethan, which was a realization that shook Kelsie to her core. What was she doing falling for a boy she'd met that day? He was handsome, of course, and she could have some fun. Nothing serious would happen. Nothing serious could ever happen.

Ethan dropped Kelsie's hand and stood with his back facing the rear wall of the house. "What do you want to talk about?"

Kelsie smiled and stepped closer. He didn't move, only watched her, and that gave her courage. "I just wanted to say thank you for being kind to me. You didn't have to."

"I got the feeling you needed it."

He was more perceptive than Kelsie had known, and probably more than anyone gave him credit for. Maybe he knew what she was going to do before she did. Kelsie stepped closer, making Ethan back himself up against the wall to leave a gap between their bodies. She raised her arms, placing her palms flat on the wall on either side of him, stood on her tiptoes and brought her lips to his.

The kiss made her knees weak and time stand still. She and Ethan both moaned, and his lips reacted to hers, sending the world spinning. It was a moment she wanted to last forever. She knew she'd have to stop kissing him at some point, for air at least. What she didn't expect was the sound of approaching footsteps. It was just her rotten luck that someone was coming to ruin her moment. Kelsie took her lips off Ethan and left her hands where they were. The entire situation had been of her making, though Ethan was a willing participant. She would take the blame. Kelsie knew that, as much as she knew she had to make a clean break from Arlo. That way, someday and somehow, she could control her own life. She wanted Ethan, but she couldn't have him past this moment. He'd go home and find someone else, someone with a real ID pass and no baggage. Kelsie would have to settle for the memory of their kiss and dazzling gazes from him to tide her over while she formed a new life for herself. It would be more difficult than anything Kelsie had ever done, and the end result would be worth it.

To Win a Proposal

Scarlet

Scarlet sat at her vanity and picked up a tube of lipstick in the only colour she wore: cherry red. It opened with a satisfying pop when she removed the lid. She puckered her lips, extended the lipstick and swiped it on. Lipstick was always the last step in her makeup routine. Normally, once it was on, she considered herself ready for whatever activity on her schedule.

Not that day. Malcolm would arrive soon to pick her up, so she needed to look better than normal. That meant dipping into her mom's jewelry. She borrowed a set of earrings and a matching necklace, which she donned after applying her lipstick.

Scarlet slid a pair of kitten heels on and grabbed her purse, which she stuck her lipstick and a compact mirror into. Malcolm couldn't see one moment of her not looking her best. All she had to do to keep him was charm him, impress him and look pretty. At least that's what her mom had said.

It hadn't worked up to that point. Scarlet had never suffered such humiliation as when Malcolm had outright told her, to her face in public, he would never marry her. Some time and perspective had granted her clarity that this was a minor setback and that she must redouble her efforts.

The one thing Scarlet was clear on, knew for certain, was that some Apartment District girl, bony and dishevelled, was not going to take Malcolm from her. He would see that whatever he felt for the girl was pity, nothing more and nothing important enough to base his future on.

Even the girl had agreed. She'd been the one to convince Malcolm to go on dates with Scarlet. The only downside in Scarlet's view was that he had to go on an equal number of dates with that girl to the ones he went on with Scarlet. It had been a necessary concession to ensure he'd agree. At least the comparison would help him realize how perfect Scarlet was for him. Boring, pity dates out of a misguided sense of charity had to pale in comparison. What could he have in common with one of the City's poor?

A muffled knock on the front door of her house brought Scarlet out of her musings. Malcolm was here, on time as he always was. Scarlet, as she always did, made him wait. Not too long, only for a minute or two. In public she never had that discipline. When her parents weren't watching, Scarlet preferred to drape herself over Malcolm. Guards were easy to pay off with her parents' money, if one ever made an issue of it.

Once she'd double checked her outfit, hair and make up in her full-length mirror, Scarlet opened her bedroom door and made her way downstairs.

Her mom had let Malcolm in, and he stood in the foyer bathed in golden sunlight streaming through the glass door. He was attractive, but his looks were just a bonus to Scarlet. She wanted him for his money, for the influence his parents had, and because Malcolm was the only boy at school that ever paid her any attention. The rest glanced past her to other, less abrasive girls. That was one of the kinder rumours that had reached her ears when someone thought she couldn't hear. They called her mean, shallow and catty, among other things. Scarlet brushed it all aside. Highschool wouldn't be her peak, nor should it. Someday she would have power and prestige, neither of which would depend on the opinions of her fellow students. They were relative nobodies, only attending her school because their parents could afford the tuition.

Malcolm glanced Scarlet's way as she descended the stairs. "You look beautiful, Scarlet." There was no malice in his eyes or tone, but there was no affection either. It wounded her that he looked at that Apartment District girl he was so fond of with more care than he looked at her. In time, the correct decision would become clear to him.

Scarlet took the compliment, knowing her didn't mean it in the way she wanted him to. She tipped her lips into a coy grin and met his eyes. She wanted more. "More beautiful than any other girl you know?" He would know whom she was implying.

Scarlet saw his shoulders tense and his eyes darken. If his answer was yes, it would be an obvious lie.

"No," he said, having the nerve to tell her the truth.

Scarlet pursed her lips, her eyes blazing. She'd known the truth, yet for him to actually say it was an insult.

His eyes stayed on her with a challenge, daring her to call him out. "My mom in her wedding pictures is more beautiful."

Scarlet forced a laugh. "I suppose I can settle for second place behind your mom until our wedding day." His words could've been true, might've been true. Sons were entitled to have bias towards their moms, but she knew what he really meant. He thought his charity case was more beautiful.

Mentioning their future wedding was a risk for Scarlet. He hadn't been perceptive in the past. At least this time he didn't outright rebuke her.

He shifted his weight on his feet and shoved his hands into his jacket pockets. "Should we go? I don't want to lose our reservation."

"Yes. I'm eager to have you to myself." She strutted out of her house and towards Malcolm's car. He could take her remark however he wanted. At least in the car she would have him alone.

Scarlet wasn't the type of girl to let herself into a car when her date could do it for her, so she walked to the passenger side and waited for Malcolm to pull her door open and close it behind her once she climbed in.

When Malcolm started the car and drove away from her house, Scarlet rested her hand on his thigh and rubbed circled with her thumb. "Isn't it nice to be alone?" she purred, leaning over to place her mouth close to his ear. "We don't have to worry about some Apartment District nobody ruining our date this time."

Malcolm shifted his leg, freeing it from under Scarlet's hand. He didn't take his eyes off the road for even a split second to look at her. "You're right. No one will ruin this date."

She leaned back on her seat and smirked. This was a small victory, which she would take as something to build on. Soon enough, she would have Malcolm planning his proposal to her. It was so close; she could almost envision the jewelry she'd pick out and hint at for him to buy. However, there was still work to do, and one adversary to take down.

"I'm sure we'll have a fantastic time. Much better than whatever you do with your charity case. You must be tired of her by now."

Malcolm exhaled his breath in a huff. "If you want me to be nice to you, don't insult her. It's not a good look."

Scarlet jutted her chin up. "I was only speaking the truth. You can't truly have real feelings for her. You and I are a much better match." Sometime soon he would see that. He had to. His infatuation with the Apartment District girl wouldn't last.

"On paper that might be true," Malcolm said, handing Scarlet another small victory. "Yet love isn't logical. It doesn't care how similar two people's upbringings are."

Scarlet hadn't known he was sentimental enough to marry for love. It was such a fleeting, silly thing. She wanted Malcolm because he didn't gossip about her, not because she loved him. He was her prize to win, and if she grew to love him, that would be a bonus. Scarlet didn't lose and wasn't going to start now. "Courtship applications do. You can't be naïve enough to think the Government would grant you one with her."

Malcom moved his shoulders in a small shrug as he pulled into the parking lot and steered towards a space near the door. "I don't pretend to know what they'd do. I wish I had your confidence about it."

Scarlet unbuckled her seatbelt and waited for Malcolm to exit his car and open her door. "It doesn't take confidence to see the obvious."

Malcolm climbed out of the car and walked around to open her door without answering her remark. Scarlet wanted him to desire her, and he was only being polite because he had to. The date wasn't ruined yet, nor was it going the way she'd dreamed it would. She walked at his side to the restaurant entrance and kept quiet as he gave his name to the maître d'.

At least the restaurant was romantic with soft lighting and intimate tables set with sparkling glasses and polished cutlery. The menu was small and pricey, just the way Scarlet preferred. What was the point in eating out if not to flaunt how much money she had? That and it kept her from having to cook.

Their table was small, only two seats across from each other with a jarred candle in the middle for ambiance. Scarlet rested her menu on the table and leaned forward, bringing herself closer to Malcolm.

He caught her gaze and set down his own menu, looking back at her with an expression that gave away nothing. It wasn't how he looked at his charity case, and he might never look at Scarlet that way. She could settle with him looking at her any way that wasn't with contempt, disgust or hate. Anything else was fine. Trapping him in a Courtship and marriage might make him resent her someday, but by then he'd have no way out. Scarlet could live on her victory and be satisfied.

Scarlet ran her finger along the rim of her glass. "This place is so romantic. I love eating by candlelight."

Malcolm lifted on eyebrow. "Is that why you chose it? For the atmosphere?"

Scarlet flashed what she hoped was a seductive grin. "Well, they also make fantastic food. I'm sure you'll love it. We can come on our anniversary every year once we're married."

A crease formed between Malcolm's brows, and his lips turned down in a frown. "You shouldn't talk like that's a forgone conclusion. I haven't told you my decision."

"But you have made it?"

"I know what decision I want to make." He continued before she could ask what that decision was. "I haven't made it yet. You'll know when I have. Please don't pester me about it."

Scarlet let the issue drop. It was enough, for the time being, that he hadn't outright stated that he wasn't choosing her. That was progress compared to their first date.

Scarlet ordered the most expensive item on the menu and a fizzy, fruity soda. Her tastes had to be more in line with Malcolm's than his charity case's. It only made sense for them to get married, considering all the things they had in common. He would see it before too long.

When the food came, Scarlet overplayed her enjoyment by letting out moans of pleasure, rolling her eyes and tilting her head back. She would perform her way into making him want her. The trouble was, Malcolm didn't do anything more than glance at her as he ate his meal.

Scarlet refused to believe he found her unattractive and undesirable. She was pretty, had impeccable taste, and had money to spare. What more could he want? If he'd had attraction for boys, she would've understood, yet he had clear feelings for his charity case. Why didn't he want her?

At the end of the meal, Scarlet paid her share. That's what rich girls did to prove they didn't need boyfriends to take care of them. It was also a message to Malcolm that she wasn't after his money, at least not entirely.

Other couples in the restaurant held hands as they walked to the door. Scarlet saw them as she waited for Malcolm to pay his bill. When he finished, Scarlet reached out and grabbed his hand. He tried to tug his hand away, but she tightened her grip and plastered on a smile she knew didn't reach her eyes. Malcolm was making things difficult for her. "This is a date. We should act like it. Don't you think?"

"You know we shouldn't."

Scarlet wanted to scream at how serious he sounded and how resistant he was being. Being on a date with her was supposed to make him happy, and here he was acting like he was tolerating it and nothing more. She cursed herself for not realizing sooner that his charity case had coerced him into supporting her little cause, but that served as Scarlet's leverage. "If you're not enjoying my company, we don't have to go on other dates, but I'll tell my father exactly why he shouldn't meet with you. What's it going to be, Malcolm?"

He closed his eyes for a moment, and his lips moved as if he was speaking to himself. There were no audible words, and Scarlet wasn't an expert lip reader, so she could only guess at what he was telling himself.

"I'll be nicer to you, Scarlet," he said. "Though I can't promise frequent dates."

Scarlet mentally kicked herself for not insisting on a set number of dates as part of their deal. She'd assumed he'd become so enraptured with her that it wouldn't take many dates for him to propose. He was harder to woo than she'd thought, and it was possible that her charms weren't as effective as she believed. "I can accept that, if I don't have to go too long before seeing you again."

Malcolm gave a hollow chuckle. "You see me all the time. We go to school together."

Scarlet pressed her lips into an exaggerated pout and fluttered her eyelashes. "That's not what I meant. I want you all to myself."

Malcolm started walking to the door, bringing Scarlet along with him as she kept her tight grip on his hand. "I know."

It was still light outside when they exited the restaurant, which was much too early to head home. "Take me dancing." It wasn't a suggestion, and she left him no choice.

His eyebrows moved together, forming a crease again, and he yanked his hand away. "We won't have much time."

Scarlet kept her hands on her sides, considering they were outside in public. "Any time is enough as long as we're together." Under the neon lights of a dance floor and the loud music, she would have Malcolm where she wanted him. He'd have to get near her. City dance floors were small and intimate. Only the young and wealthy frequented them, and the staff were known to be discreet, especially when tipped well. No one would call a guard on them if they kissed in that environment. It was just what Malcolm needed to loosen up, and Scarlet would show him how much fun she was.

Malcolm peered at her, seeming to weigh something over in his mind. When he came to a decision, he opened her door and watched her climb in. "We can go, if that's what you really want."

"It is." He was finally coming around to seeing the joys of spending time with her. If she'd been younger, she might've squealed, but she remained composed as Malcolm closed her door and walked around to get in the car.

As he pulled the car out of the parking lot, he cast a glance on Scarlet. "I'll take you anywhere you want, but I want a meeting with your father."

Scarlet waved her hand in dismissal. His remark was a nuisance, and she didn't need a reminder of what she'd promised. "You'll get it. I haven't forgotten the deal we agreed on."

"I mean before Clinic Day. I want it as soon as possible."

Scarlet laughed. He thought taking her to a dance floor would be enough to give up her leverage? It was all she had that kept him around. "Why should I arrange that? I'm no fool."

Malcolm tightened his grip on the steering wheel so much his knuckles went white. "Because I can make my choice tonight, and never see you again. If you truly want me to consider you as my Courtship partner, you'll do this for me."

Scarlet folded her arms in her lap and tried to meet his eyes in the mirror. He had to have lost his sense to believe she would agree to that. "What's to stop you from leaving me as soon as you meet him?"

"You have my word I'll go on dates with you until I make my choice. Please, Scarlet, don't force me to make it tonight."

Perhaps if she granted him this, it would further her goal. A little compromise could be good in a relationship when implemented correctly. "Very well. I'll arrange it and send a note with the details." That placated

Malcolm, and he kept his word by taking her to a dance floor.

Scarlet grabbed his hand upon exiting the car and flitted her way to the line, tugging him along. The bouncer nodded and cleared the way when Scarlet and Malcolm showed him their ID cards for scanning. Entry to expensive entertainment was another perk of having money. Scarlet saw nothing wrong with flaunting her privilege. Why should she be ashamed of it?

The inside of the building was dimly lit by pulsing neon lights, and a DJ machine played catchy, upbeat songs only the wealthy had time, money and capability to produce. The poor had no budget for entertainment; this music wasn't for them. It was created for and funded by the rich.

Scarlet led Malcolm onto the floor under the pulsing lights. He had an eerie look here, appearing less golden under the neon bulbs. Scarlet was sure her own hair looked duller, but it resembled ashes at the best of times. There was something attractive about Malcolm with the lights casting shadows on his face and cutting it at harsher angles. He was Scarlet's here, not the golden boy an Apartment District girl pined after.

Scarlet twined her wrists behind his neck, pulling his face down. She stood on her tiptoes to press her lips against his. The kiss sent bubbles through her body, making her feel as light as air. Warmth followed, starting from her core and spreading to her extremities. This was what she'd been waiting for. Her knees didn't go weak, and the ground remained steady below her feet, but Scarlet was too strong for those physical reactions.

She was wearing a genuine smile when she pulled away, and he tried to match it. Her mind was still clear enough to notice it didn't reach his eyes. She refused to entertain the notion that she was bad at kissing, and the alternative was he felt nothing for her. That was the better option, though still not ideal.

"You know we shouldn't do that in public."

"We can get away with it here. You worry too much." She kept her hold on him and started to sway to the beat of the song that played. He would have no choice now except to dance with her.

Malcolm placed his hands at her waist, keeping a loose grip. At least he was touching her.

He raised an eyebrow. "Don't tell me you like paying fines."

Scarlet had never paid for one with her own money. The idea was ridiculous. "My parents pay them. Don't yours?"

He tossed his head and exhaled a sigh. "No. I do."

Scarlet's parents gave her anything and everything she asked for. All the money she spent was theirs to begin with. She couldn't imagine Malcolm having to pay his own way. "How unfortunate for you."

Malcolm looked at Scarlet with hardened eyes. He wasn't taking her pity. "My parents aren't like yours. I do a lot for myself."

If that was true, Scarlet would let him keep doing it in their marriage. Why should she do housework and pay for fines when he was used to doing it already? It made her want him more, knowing she'd never have to worry about such trivial things. "That's another reason why we make such a good match. I've never had to do much of anything for myself. You can take care of all that for me."

Malcolm exhaled a sigh and took a step back from her, letting go of her waist and wriggling out of her grip. "Do you want a husband or a servant? Marriages are meant to be partnerships."

Scarlet stepped towards him. He wasn't going to flee from her in this place, and she knew he wouldn't strand her here to walk home. "I want you as my husband."

He didn't move, which Scarlet took as another small victory, and she stepped even closer to plant another kiss on his lips and rest her hands on his chest. "Just give me a chance, Malcolm. I'll prove how good of a wife I can be to you."

With the minimal distance between them, he had to meet her eyes, and she saw him swallow before responding. "You have your chance."

His words didn't come with a kiss, yet they were enough for Scarlet for the time being. The rest of their time dancing dragged by, and Scarlet grew bored. She let Malcolm take her home as the sun went down, and he drove fast, with a tight grip on the steering wheel and no words for Scarlet. Perhaps she should've let him drive her home earlier and received a more satisfying ending to their date. When they reached her house, she had to let herself out of the car and barely got a wave from him as he drove off, and she walked to her door alone. He didn't even say goodnight.

Scarlet went to her room and screamed into her pillow. Malcolm was resisting her and her advances at every turn, though he hadn't broken any part of the deal they'd made. Still, she knew his charity case must've gotten hooks into him for him to resist Scarlet. She made every move. Not once did he initiate a kiss, a hand hold, or even offer her a compliment after the one delivered when he picked her up. It was like he didn't want to touch her.

Scarlet loathed feeling undesirable, though there was no value in self-pity. She took some deep breaths to calm herself, picked herself up, and went to her father's office to make good on what she'd promised Malcolm. "Dad?" she called as she knocked on the door, and he turned from his chair to look at her. "I need a favour."

Her dad was easy to convince to find time to meet with Malcolm and his Apartment District girl. Scarlet didn't care whether their little cause had any success. The food laws worked fine in her opinion. If the poor couldn't afford food, that wasn't her problem.

She set the meeting up to show Malcolm she could be nice to him and support what he cared about, and to prove to his Apartment District girl who was the better match for him. With her out of the way, Malcolm would belong to Scarlet. It couldn't be that difficult for his charity case to feel out of place and remove herself from the equation. She was the one thing in Scarlet's way, and this would be a simple way to resolve the issue. If it embarrassed her rival, that would only be a bonus.

Scarlet slept soundly with a smile on her face. Soon Malcolm would give her the perfect proposal and gift, and they'd have an extravagant wedding with all the gossipers from school in attendance to witness her triumph. Becoming Mrs. Connor would stop the rumours. They'd all be jealous of her then.

Her dream was so close, she could feel it. All Scarlet had to do was charm Malcolm and scare off one, poor, insignificant girl. In time, Malcolm would forget about the pity he'd had for one of the City's unfortunate and might even laugh about it with Scarlet. That would be the perfect ending and make all her hard work worth it.

An Opportunity

Malcolm

Malcolm gripped the glass in his hand tighter. *Water*. It was always water these days. He'd cut costs wherever he could over the past few years, and it wasn't enough. "You think I should do it?"

His friend, Jack Birch, sat across from him at a table in the back corner of Catsy's diner in Apartment District 6 that Amelia had frequented, before their marriage, their two children and the awful, uncurable sickness that had taken her from them. Jack took a sip of his own water. "I said it's a great opportunity for the Rebel Cause. I didn't say whether you should do it."

Malcolm sighed. "Amelia would be so disappointed."

Jack nodded, his eyes faraway. He'd been Amelia's friend before Malcolm's. "If she was alive, we wouldn't be discussing this."

If Amelia had lived, Scarlet Everbee wouldn't have requested a meeting. Malcolm had attended with intentions of telling her to go away. Just because Amelia was dead three years now didn't mean he'd reconsider marrying Scarlet.

Marriage hadn't been her intention at all. Malcolm had sat in stunned disbelief as she pitched him a job, with accommodations, generous salary and power. Her only nonnegotiable catch was that he give up everything tied to Amelia, including his children. Malcolm had told her no, he would never do such a thing, and Scarlet had patted his hand and said she'd wait a week for his final answer, once he'd thought it over.

It was a terrible thing to do to his children: five-year-old Valerie and three-year-old Henry. Every instinct in Malcolm's body screamed to run from this. He'd never been one to crave power or control. The truth was, in his grief over Amelia, Malcolm had lost his job and spent through most of his savings. There was little left after paying her medical bills. If he turned down Scarlet's offer, he'd have to sell his house, move to one of the poorer Apartment Districts and find a menial job, which might still not provide for his children. He'd tried to find a job for a while now, with no luck. Maybe Scarlet had blacklisted him.

"You have to think of your kids," Jack said.

"You think I'm not?" Malcolm downed the water in his glass in one gulp and set it down with a thud. "What could I do to them that's worse than this?"

Jack gave him a pitying look. "Move them to a grungy apartment where they have to share a bedroom and starve while the neighbours judge them for having each other."

Malcolm bit back his groan. His children didn't have the life he'd envisioned for them, and he saw no way to provide while staying in their life. His parents had helped where they could, but Malcolm needed to fix his own problems. "It might be best if they grew up with someone that could give them everything they deserve. That's no longer me."

"You're acting like you can never see them again."

"Scarlet said I can't. It will be like they never existed." The thought of it made Malcolm's heart shatter. How could Scarlet be so cruel, jealous and bitter to demand such a thing?

"You've gotten so dramatic. Don't you remember how to handle Scarlet?"

"It's been years. I stopped worrying about it when Amelia and I got our

Courtship." Once Malcolm had left school, and stopped seeing her in the hallways, he hadn't thought about Scarlet much at all, if ever.

"Just tell her what she wants to hear and act the part. I'll keep an eye on your kids and update you."

As a teenager, Malcolm had known how to diffuse Scarlet and flatter her ego. It had been exhausting then, and he didn't relish the idea of regaining those skills. "How?"

Jack downed the rest of his water. "While you've been in mourning, I've been making connections and helping Arlo Fenn. The Rebel Cause has eyes everywhere except high up in the Government. It'll be easy enough to put a watch on your kids."

It dawned on Malcolm then why Jack hadn't told him to turn down Scarlet's offer. "You want me to fill that gap."

Jack lifted his shoulders in a shrug. "Scarlet handed us the opportunity. If you take her up on it and help us, you'll do more for Valerie and Henry than you ever could by moving them to an Apartment District."

Malcolm closed his eyes. His parents had always supported change in the City, had funded deliveries to the Colony and hadn't batted an eye when he'd helped Amelia overturn the old food laws. Amelia had wanted change desperately, almost as much as she'd wanted him. He could almost hear her telling him to do it, that they couldn't waste this chance, just like she'd convinced him to go on dates with Scarlet in exchange for a meeting with Scarlet's father. Yet he couldn't believe Amelia would want him to leave their children. "If Amelia was alive, she'd never let me do this, but she's not here to be angry. Valerie and Henry are the ones who'll have to forgive me someday."

He didn't feel worthy of being their father or of having their forgiveness. This could be a way to prove himself, even if it meant not being there in person to see them grow up. Surely, it couldn't take that long to help Jack. They'd overturned the food laws in a few months, and there was no specific aim this time. He could go, make some money, give Jack some intel and leave Scarlet and the rest behind. Amelia, if she was able, couldn't object to that sacrifice. "I'll tell Scarlet I'll do it."

...

Malcolm set foot inside his house and wobbled from the impact of his children running at him to hug his legs. He bent down, scooped them up and ruffled their hair. Somehow, both Valerie and Henry had inherited his hair, eye and skin colour, though here were bits of Amelia in their features, for those that knew her enough to see them.

Malcolm held his children close as he carried them deeper into the house. He'd already sold the furniture they didn't absolutely need, and he'd emptied Amelia's former office. Keeping it as she left it would've stuck his mind in a grief-stricken, lonely place. Valerie and Henry had been his focus for the three years she'd been gone.

"Daddy," Valerie tugged on his sleeve. "I want pancakes."

Malcolm set his children down in the kitchen doorway. Valerie always wanted pancakes. "Maybe for breakfast tomorrow. Why don't you go play with Henry?"

With them in the next room, Malcolm threw together a meal. If it wasn't for the ration system, they would've starved. That was a lasting gift from Amelia.

Malcolm never could get her out of his head, and thoughts of her came stronger now that he'd decided to take Scarlet's offer. After the meal, and his children's bedtime, Malcolm gathered up paperwork, jewelry, photos and a metal box. Some of the items had been Amelia's: her ID card, her courtship jewelry and wedding ring, and her proof of parentage card for Valerie and Henry. To those, he added their marriage license, Courtship papers, a picture of Amelia holding Valerie and Henry, the latest picture he'd had taken of himself with his children, his proof of parentage card, their child permits, his wedding ring, and the gold pin in the shape of a C from his father. He had to protect Amelia's memory from Scarlet.

With the pile gathered, he went into Amelia's office. It was at the back of the house, hidden from the front windows by the staircase, which was perfect for his purpose. No prying neighbours could see in to detect anyone retrieving the items. He walked to the back corner, crouched and pried up a floor tile. Digging a hole under the floor would've been easier with a power tool, but he only had a chisel he'd bought on the way home. Anything else would've made too much noise.

Malcolm had never been one to work with his hands, having come from a wealthy family, but there was nowhere else to store things he couldn't part with that Scarlet wouldn't find. So, he chipped away at the material under the floor tile until he had a hole he could fit the box in. The dust was all over him and the undisturbed tiles around him, and his hands ached, but the mess and the pain were well worth it.

He was almost proud when he tucked the items into the box, put the lid on top, re-laid the tile and cleaned the dust. No one would know he'd moved it or stored anything under the floor. The only person that would need to was Jack.

If something happened and he was away from his children for an extended time, Jack could show them the pictures. Henry was so little, Malcolm feared Henry would forget him. Even Valerie, at five, could forget. It was better to store proof for their sake, as well as his and Amelia's. He couldn't let Scarlet find them, or she would burn the papers and send the jewelry to be refashioned into something else. It would effectively erase the history of his family, and that would crush him more than leaving his children. At least they would have a chance at a good life this way.

Malcolm didn't waste time on contacting Scarlet. The morning after making his decision, he sent her a message requesting a meeting. Her response came the following day, and he set out to the café she'd agreed on. There was a time, in his youth, he'd eaten out frequently, either with Scarlet or his parents, and later with Amelia. He'd relished Amelia's awe of the meals she hadn't had to cook with whatever meagre ingredients her parents had been able to afford. It was a drastic difference from Scarlet who took everything for granted.

She still did. When he walked in, the greeter took him to a table in a secluded corner of the café where Scarlet sat with a coffee and a strawberry scone. Her brought her cup to her lips and drank a sip. "I still love seeing you walk in."

Malcolm sat and heaved a sigh. "I know you wanted us to marry once, but I can't, Scarlet."

Scarlet coughed as her sip of coffee caught in her throat. When her coughs subsided, she pursed her lips. "I would never be so desperate to demand her leftovers. Don't insult me so."

"I don't mean it as an insult. I just want to be clear that I won't accept your offer if a condition is us having any form of romantic relationship."

Scarlet dabbed her lips with a napkin and bit into her scone. "I meant it years ago when I told you that you could decide whom you married. It's your fault for choosing the wrong person. I think you should forget about her and her offspring. My offer is a compassionate one really, and a lifeline to help you reclaim the lifestyle you deserve, free from distractions and reminders of the rebel sympathizer."

"Perhaps you're right," Malcolm said, the words tasting like acid in his mouth. He was trying to do as Jack advised and tell Scarlet what she wanted to hear. "I've decided to take you up on it."

A wicked smile grew on her face. If Malcolm hadn't already fretted over the decision and been so desperate to help Jack and his children however he could, that smile might've made him pause. It was the smile of a predator knowing they'd trapped their prey. Scarlet saw herself as earning a huge victory with his one sentence.

"Excellent. Don't tell the children, or your parents. We don't need them coming looking for you or making a scene."

Malcolm should've foreseen that, but it rocked him all the same. Somehow, the situation kept getting worse. "What would you have me do? Just leave and never go back?"

"Yes. It's best for them to think you're dead. I'll have someone go by and tell them. Don't worry about anything. I'll send a message with the date and address where you can sign your contract."

Malcolm had imagined telling his family something, although he hadn't settled on what. Having them think he was dead wasn't what he wanted or thought best for them, yet Scarlet was immovable.

"They must mean nothing to you now. You cannot have ties to the rebels, and those children came from a rebel sympathizer. We'll spin this as a mistake and that you regret getting involved with a traitor who seduced you."

No matter what Scarlet said or wanted Malcolm to believe, he would never see Amelia as a traitor, yet his personal views had to remain silent and hidden. Scarlet had to think he agreed with her. "Fine."

It wasn't a decision he could back away from, which haunted him as he waited for her message during the following days. He spent the time trying to act normal around Valerie and Henry, though his heart broke every time they went to sleep. The end of each day meant he was one day closer to being out of their lives.

The waiting started to get to Malcolm, and he considered telling Scarlet to forget the whole thing. The problem was, he knew he couldn't provide for his children, and this was an opportunity to help the movement Amelia had been so passionate about. He couldn't turn it down now. So, he waited until the day he opened his front door to find a card addressed to him with a short message scrawled on the back: *Tomorrow at 2 pm, Quarter 2 business district, Street 4 café.*

Malcolm stuck the message in his pocket, closed his door and went to the phone in his office to call his parents. He couldn't leave Valerie and Henry alone, and he wanted them to be with familiar people. The other option was Amelia's parents, who'd become distant after her passing. They'd only met Henry once, in the days after his birth when Amelia lingered. Malcolm didn't want to involve them in this.

It was easy to get his parents to agree to babysit. They loved chances to do so and didn't question Malcolm when he provided no specific reason as to why.

He didn't sleep that night. Once his children were in their beds, Malcolm sat in Valerie's doorway, then later Henry's, and tried to memorize their faces. Everyone thought they were replicas of him, and there were obvious similarities, but Malcolm saw Amelia when he looked at them. He never wanted to forget Amelia's face, yet it was harder to remember with each passing day. It would only get worse when he didn't have pictures of her to look at for reminders. She was gone, never to return, and he refused to give up on her memory.

In the early hours of the morning, Malcolm left the upstairs hallway for his office. He sat at his desk, pulled a photo album off the shelf behind him and flipped through the pages. It was a partly filled album, having only pictures of him and Amelia, from when they married up to Henry's birth. He had never been able to add to it, preferring to place pictures of his children in a separate album, which he added to his desk.

Scarlet would trash the albums if given the chance, he knew that, and he'd already stored a few important pictures away that might be necessary in the future. There was little he could do about the rest other than hand them over to Jack. If he left early enough, he would have time before meeting Scarlet. They weren't vital pictures, not useful for anything other than sentiment, unlike the few he'd hidden in Amelia's office, and the albums were too big to fit in the box.

Perhaps he was too tied to the past, but he wanted to preserve as much of Amelia and her memory as he could. Certainly, he didn't want everything of hers in Scarlet's hands. That would only lead to destruction fueled by the burning desire for revenge Scarlet had possessed for years.

With a plan formed on what to do with the photo albums, Malcolm went into the kitchen to make pancakes. If it was his last morning with his children for the near future, he would give them what Valerie always wanted. Henry offered no such opinions on meals, though Malcolm suspected he might in time. Henry would only let his older sister get her way for so long.

Whatever happened, Scarlet had sworn that Valerie and Henry would have each other. That would be a small comfort, both to them and Malcolm.

Malcolm tried to appear normal as he ate breakfast with his children and told them his parents would stay with them for the day. As young as Valerie and Henry were, they didn't think to question why. It was almost too easy to get them excited over it.

When breakfast was over, Malcolm packed a satchel with his ID card, some clothes he didn't want to leave behind and the photo albums. His parents arrived as he buckled the bag closed and slid the strap over his shoulder. His stomach was in knots, and his heart pounded in his chest as he greeted his parents, hugged and kissed his children, told them he loved them, and walked out of his house for what would be the last time before his life changed completely all over again.

The first major change in his life had been the day he'd met Amelia. He thought of her as he walked to the bus headed towards the Apartment Districts. This was the best thing to do.

He feared, of course, that in playing along with distancing himself from Amelia's memory and their children, he would start to believe they meant nothing to him. It was essential that he always remembered why he'd agreed to do this.

Jack was home with his wife Dina and two-year-old daughter Molly when Malcolm got to their apartment. Molly peeked from behind Jack's legs, her green eyes the only similarity to Dina. The rest of her looked like Jack. Jack scooped her up and held her on his hip.

"Today's the day?" he asked Malcolm.

Malcolm nodded. He set down his satchel, opened the buckle and pulled out the albums. "I'm hoping you'll store these for me. They wouldn't fit in Amelia's office with everything else I hid."

Dina had hurt almost as much as Malcolm when Amelia passed, having been Amelia's best friend since meeting her in preschool. She looked at Malcolm now with a mix of pity and sadness. "We'll find somewhere for them.

Anything to keep Scarlet from completely erasing Amelia."

"I'm grateful," Malcolm said. "I couldn't bear the thought of what Scarlet would do."

Jack carried Molly to her room. "You think she'll sell the house?" he asked when he came back.

Malcolm sighed. "I put it in my parents' name without telling them. She won't be able to sell it, nor will she tell my parents. Scarlet would rather let it fall to ruin. You can take whatever you want from it. The key's in the same place."

Jack met Malcolm's eyes and dipped his head. "I'll keep an eye on it."

Dina closed her eyes and shook her head. "The bigger concern should be the children."

Malcolm too had more concerns over them than his house, but he couldn't control what happened. "I'm sure they'll go to the Foster Centre. Scarlet said they'll stay together."

"Arlo has eyes there," Jack said. "We'll keep track of them."

Dina reached for Jack's hand and clutched it tight like it was her tether. "I wish we could do more."

No one Malcolm knew could. If he had only one child, his parents could've applied for a second child permit and adopted them. With two, that was impossible. Amelia's parents didn't have enough money for the permit, and he didn't want to separate his children. "It isn't your responsibility, Dina."

"He's right," Jack said. "We can't barely afford to care for Molly, let alone more kids."

Dina sighed, and tears pooled in the corners of her eyes. "Amelia would be heartbroken over this, though I suppose there's nothing to be done now."

Malcolm winced at the mention of Amelia. If she were around to be heartbroken, he wouldn't be in the situation. "No. I'm doing all I can. What's best is for them to live with people who can take care of them and provide for them."

Dina swiped her tears with her thumb. "Of course."

Malcolm closed his satchel and placed the strap over his shoulder. "Thank you both. Not everyone would take such great risks."

Jack gave Malcolm a knowing grin. "You're the one taking the biggest risk, which I talked you into. The least we can do is store some photos and watch over your house and kids. Now get going before Scarlet thinks you've changed your mind."

Malcolm made his goodbyes and left the apartment building for the bus. Before Amelia's death, he'd never ridden the bus. The buses were notorious for being slow, stopping often, and crowded. It had been uncomfortable the first few times, and now it was normal to him. He'd gotten used to the jostling for seats or handholds and to keeping a tight hold on whatever belongings he carried. Selling his car had provided him more time with his children thanks to money desperately needed for medical bills. It hadn't been enough.

This trip on the bus was like any other, and the bus emptied as it approached the rich Quarters and progressed through them. Malcolm was the only passenger to get off at his stop. He stood on the road and inhaled a deep breath to gather his courage. It was too late to change his mind now, and doing so wouldn't solve his money problems.

With his nerves settled, and his determination high, he walked to the address Scarlet had provided on her note. It was a bright and quaint café with large windows and a striped awning. The door had bells that rung when he pushed it open and stepped inside, alerting the staff to his presence.

Scarlet was sitting at a table with a mug and a pile of papers. She didn't so much as look up, though Malcolm assumed she knew he was there. He walked over with his heart racing and told himself he had to do this.

Scarlet didn't even glance his way as he arrived. She lifted her mug and drank a sip of the steaming, brown liquid in it. "I was just starting to worry you weren't coming."

Malcolm took the seat across from her. "The bus got here as quickly as it could." Scarlet had never ridden a bus, had no clue of how inefficient and slow they were. He didn't try to explain.

She choked on her drink, making her cough into her napkin. "You'll never ride that again. It's for the poor."

Malcolm ignored the derision and judgement in her voice. Speaking his distaste wouldn't help matters. "And how else will I get around? I sold my car."

Scarlet patted his hand. "We'll discuss details after you sign." She slid the papers and a pen across the table and locked eyes with him. "First, you must understand that this is a permanent arrangement. You cannot go back to *her* children."

Malcolm had hope that the Rebel Cause would have a say in how permanent this predicament would be, and that he would have a reunion with his children, not that he let Scarlet in on any of that. "I know."

He took the pen and brought the pages closer to pour through them. Signing without reading was an option, though not one he wanted to take. It was always better to go into a deal with an idea of what he was agreeing to. That way Scarlet couldn't blindside him later with stipulations he was unaware of.

Most of the document was a standard contract. The only parts that stood out were the requirements of secrecy, though those clauses fit with the idea of the Government he had. They also weren't ones he would adhere strictly to, by way of sharing intel with Jack.

When he got to the end, he put the pen tip on the dotted line and scrawled his name. His last name didn't feel like his anymore. Joining the Government in exchange of his children was a betrayal to his family name, which had led him to leave behind the pin his father had gifted him on his wedding day. Someday, somehow, he would get it to Henry. His son was more deserving of the family name than Malcolm would ever be again.

Scarlet broke into a cold, wide grin when the papers were signed. She'd never been capable of showing joy for anyone, just glee at others' misfortune. This seemed more predatory and vindictive, like she'd duped Malcolm into giving her a victory.

"I always knew you'd make the right decision," she cooed. "Your life will be much better now that your past mistakes are forgotten."

Malcolm could only nod his head. He'd done it. There was no going back. That reality hit him as he left the café with Scarlet and walked to the car she'd parked along the road. He supposed some people might've felt grateful or victorious having been gifted this opportunity. Not Malcolm. This wasn't the path he wanted to take or would ever have taken if he'd had a better choice. His mind swam with thoughts of his children and the terrible news they'd soon receive, but this was an opportunity the Rebel Cause needed, and he was the only one who could take it. That was the thought he clung to and built his resolve around as Scarlet drove him to his new life.

The Escape

Valerie

Valerie sat on the bench outside the headmistress's office. The trouble she was in this time wasn't that big, or she would've been summoned to the director. While she waited, she let her blonde hair drape over her hunched shoulders and crossed her arms.

She'd been at the Foster Centre for six years now, more than half of her life. Her father's face was blurry in her memory, but she remembered the day he died. He'd hugged her and her little brother Henry on his way out the door and said he loved them. That was the last time Valerie saw her father, and no one had taken her to his funeral, if he'd had one. Those were rare and expensive with Government mandated cremations and ashes used in the greenhouses.

The Foster Centre was where she lived now, though it wasn't home. Home had been bright, spacious and nice smelling, with tasty food and bright flowers in a yard of her family's own and a bedroom just for Valerie. The Foster Centre was dark and foreboding, with bars on the windows, shared dormitories, and a wall separating the boys' side of the building from the girls'.

Kids at the Foster Centre weren't let outside on the chance one would make an escape attempt. Valerie wouldn't run away, not without her brother Henry. Nor would she charm any family into adopting her, even if that would free her from this place. That's how she winded up on the headmistress's bench again.

The stern assistant, Miss Kenson, tapped her foot, tsked and shook her head at Valerie. "Miss Connor, the headmistress will see you now. You know where to go."

Valerie rose from the bench, walked to the headmistress's office and entered the room when Miss Kenson opened the door. When it closed behind Valerie, she glanced around the small room.

In front of the desk stood Mrs. Cleeson, the headmistress. She wore a tailored business suit and her hair in a tight bun. Today there was pink lipstick on her lips. In the past, Valerie had feared Mrs. Cleeson. Not anymore. Countless visits to this office had dulled the terror Mrs. Cleeson struck into other girls for Valerie.

Mrs. Cleeson walked over and circled Valerie with disdain. "You've been quite the bit of trouble. Another couple passing on you. I don't understand it. The instructors tell me you cooperate in class and are obedient, yet all our hard work goes away as soon as you have the chance to leave here. Tell me, Valerie, do you want to stay here?"

No. Valerie wanted nothing of the sort, but she couldn't leave without Henry. Admitting that would bring her worse punishment than anything Mrs. Cleeson ever did to her. It might even end with her hauled before the director. She wasn't eager to earn more lashes from his belt. One session of that had been enough. "This is the only home I remember." A lie, of course.

Mrs. Cleeson stopped circling, pursed her lips and narrowed her eyes. "This isn't your home. You're here to learn skills that will make you desirable and valuable to a childless couple looking to adopt. Evidently, that's something you haven't grasped."

"I understand, Mrs. Cleeson, but maybe no one wants me." She didn't care whether anyone did. Her parents were dead, and the Foster Centre kept Henry away from her. He was her only family left. If her grandparents were alive, they couldn't take both Henry and her. Only one set of her grandparents could afford a second child permit, and she knew they never would've chosen between Valerie and Henry in that way. Sending them both to the Foster Centre at least made them equal.

"No, they certainly do not. This was your last chance, which I was already reluctant to give you."

Valerie's jaw dropped, and she snapped it shut as panic rose in her stomach. "Are – are you going to kick me out?" Her voice trembled, and she hated herself for showing that bit of weakness. How could she help Henry if she was cast out onto the streets for a guard to round up? Prison had to be worse than here.

Mrs. Cleeson scoffed. "You'll stay here and be put to work. Outside of school classes, which the Government mandates we teach you, you'll occupy your time doing labour."

Valerie tried to look meek and repentant, even though it was a victory. No amount of physical work could be worse than being further separated from her brother. She left Mrs. Cleeson's office with her head bowed and hid her smile.

The Foster Centre staff wasted no time in arranging work for her. As soon as she was in the hallway, the housekeep thrust a broom and dustpan into Valerie's hands.

Valerie didn't get a maid's uniform or salary, and her duties were those the paid cleaners didn't want to do, yet she felt like a maid. Of course, they never let her into the boys' half of the building or the hallway leading to it.

Her attempts at sneaking her way to Henry ensured she was never to go near the connecting doors again.

Valerie had bided her time for years now, and she had to be patient longer. With her new punishment, the staff kept her busier than ever and under stricter watch. At least they weren't shoving her in front of potential adopters anymore. It had always made Valerie feel like a piece of furniture being sold off, and the primping the staff had put her through beforehand was torture. Valerie had always messed up her hair and wiped off the makeup as soon as she was in the waiting room.

Now, as a maid, Valerie wore her hair tied back, and her clothes grew threadbare and dingy from the amount of time she spent on her knees and in dusty corners.

The other girls in her dormitory snickered and gossiped about Valerie. It didn't bother her. None of them were her friends or even her age. The months ticked by, passing Valerie's twelfth birthday with barely a thought from her. No one did anything for birthdays in this place.

She had vague memories of her fifth birthday, when her father had still been alive. The specifics had left her long ago, but Valerie remembered the doll he'd gifted her. She'd been holding it when the Foster Centre agents had come for her and Henry and ripped it, then later Henry, out of her arms.

The Foster Centre, and the people working in it, were cruel, yet they were familiar to Valerie. She knew the rules and how much she could get away with. Turning twelve was a reminder to Valerie that she'd failed for another year. Henry's cries from the last time she'd seen him haunted her dreams, and she threw herself into her chores to drown out the memories and her guilt.

On the next day prospective couples came to meet eligible children to adopt, Valerie got a rare break from her work and was alone in the dormitory.

No one wanted her roaming about when she'd been banned from seeing potential adopters, so Mrs. Cleeson had ordered her to her cot until the end of the day.

Valerie hugged her knees and sighed. The sun was still high in the sky when she heard a single pair of footsteps nearing her room. She let go of her knees, sat up and turned towards the door. Her heart pounded. Maybe Mrs. Cleeson had thrust Valerie into work to distract her from whichever horrible person she'd arranged to take Valerie.

Valerie scanned the room, seeing nothing to use a weapon. Foster Centre kids were supplied clothes, a pair of shoes, toiletries kept in the bathroom and basic school items kept in the classrooms and study hall. Her shoes weren't heavy enough to wound anyone. Valerie hated feeling helpless and got to her feet. She could at least try to run when her kidnapper came.

The footsteps stopped outside the door, and the knob turned. Valerie balled her hands into fists, intending to hit her way through, when a man with chestnut hair and fair skin stepped in. He was alone.

"Valerie Connor," he said with a bright smile that reached his blue eyes. "I'm so glad you're here."

Valerie froze. No one ever looked at her with that much warmth. "Mrs. Cleeson said I wouldn't be adopted, sir."

The man's smile shrunk, and his face softened as he looked at Valerie. "Your dad sent me to take you somewhere safe. I'm his friend Jack."

Valerie scowled. She felt like a child younger than her years as she pouted with her lower lip jutting out, and her voice broke. "My father is dead." A dead man couldn't send anyone for her. Why was Jack really here?

Jack stuck his hand into his pocket and produced a picture that he passed to Valerie. It was unmistakably her and Henry with their father. She hadn't seen it in years, since before it went missing after her father's death. Was he really alive? If so, why had he waited this long to help her? Valerie got no chance to ask those questions before Jack spoke again.

"We don't have much time. The guards are changing shifts. If you gather your things quickly, we can get out unseen."

Out. This was a chance at escape offered by a man who had a picture from her father. It was also an opportunity for answers. Valerie kept her eyes on the picture. *Henry.* He needed her. "I won't leave without my brother."

Jack heaved a sigh. "He was adopted last year. We thought you knew." From his other pocket, he pulled out a file and handed it to Valerie. It was a copy of an adoption record with Henry's name and picture on it and the official stamp from the Government. He looked so much like a mini version of their father and like Valerie that she wanted to cry.

"They've told me nothing of Henry."

Jack handed her a small duffel bag. "I'm sorry. I wish there was more time, but —"

Valerie snatched the bag and shoved her few pairs of clothes in it. She darted to the connecting bathroom and emptied the contents of her cubby into the bag, tucking the picture of her family in the small pocket with her ID pass. Jack was a stranger, but he was offering her escape and had told her information on Henry. That was more than anyone had done for her in years. Her brother was gone, and there was no reason to stay.

Valerie clutched the duffel bag to her chest as she followed Jack into the hallway and to the elevator. The other girls, and most of the staff, were on the ground floor waiting room and meeting rooms with couples looking to adopt. Valerie didn't so much as glance at as she and Jack passed by after exiting the elevator.

Valerie hadn't been outside since her arrival seven years earlier, and the hot air hit her face, causing beads of sweat to form at her hairline when Jack opened the door. With a deep breath, she stepped over the threshold and into her new life.

"This way." Jack waved Valerie on as he flew down the steps, across the front walkway and through the gate left open for visiting couples.

Valerie tried to ignore the memories she had of her arrival. The Foster Centre's front yard was split in half from left to right with a large wall and wrap around fence. One side was for girls, and the other for boys. At five years old, at the edge of the road where the grounds began, workers had ripped Henry from her arms and taken him inside a separate gate from the one they'd dragged her kicking and screaming through. She hadn't seen him since.

Valerie ran after Jack, tears streaming down her face. She couldn't wipe them without letting go of her bag, and that wasn't an option.

Jack reached his truck, parked down the street, before Valerie did. He was standing at the back, bent forward and searching for something. Valerie heard a click and saw him lift the truck bed, revealing a dark crawl space underneath.

Jack gave her a lopsided, closed-lip smile. "It's not the most comfortable ride, but you can't sit in the open. I didn't get their permission to take you."

Valerie's heart thudded. He wanted her to crawl in there? "They won't care." If she'd been any other girl, the Foster Centre would call a guard and send a search party. For Valerie, they'd be glad to be rid of her, even if it meant losing her free labour.

"A guard will if one stops us."

The last thing Valerie wanted was a guard dragging her back here. She knew things at the Foster Centre would be even worse for her then, and there would be a trip to the director and his leather belt. She'd done her best to behave enough to prevent that again. With a gulp, she summoned her courage and, with Jack's help, climbed into the compartment. She lay on her back, and Jack passed in her bag, a wrapped sandwich and a water flask.

Valerie got hold of the items and gave Jack a small nod. He lowered the lid, and the latch clicked. It was so dark in the compartment that Valerie couldn't see her hand in front of her face. Her tears flowed unchecked, and she sniffled. She heard Jack close a door to the trunk and the engine come to life. As a small child, she'd ridden in her father's car, and then the Foster Centre agents had taken her and Henry in a car. Those times had been nothing like this.

Valerie hadn't thought she was scared of the dark or small spaces, but being stuck in this compartment had her pulse racing and a pit growing in her stomach. After a few minutes, her eyes adjusted. She swiped away her tears and saw faint light coming in along the edge of the compartment lid. It wasn't enough to make her space bright, but she could see the borders of the area and the shape of her bag.

Valerie grabbed the flask, pulled off the cap and gulped some of the liquid inside. Her hand shook, but the truck drove smooth, and the water found her mouth. Whatever she'd gotten herself into had to be worth it.

…

The sun was setting when the truck stopped, and Jack opened the lid. He offered her a hand and a smile. "Are you hungry?"

Valerie took his hand and his help getting out of the compartment. They were in the middle of nowhere, and the night air was warm. Her legs were weak, so Jack had to hold her up until she got her balance. She'd eaten the sandwich, and still her stomach rumbled. It hadn't been enough to keep her full. "Yes."

She sat on the ground next to Jack and ate another sandwich he handed her from a paper bag. Both sandwiches had tasted better than any food at the Foster Centre.

"I'm sorry we couldn't stop sooner," Jack said, holding his own sandwich. "I couldn't risk someone seeing you."

Valerie gulped some of her water to dislodge the peanut butter sandwich from the roof of her mouth. "Where are we going?" Jack had never told her, and there hadn't been a moment to ask.

"The Colony. You'll be safer there."

Valerie frowned. She'd never heard of the Colony. All that remained of the world, according to the Foster Centre, was the City and the Outskirts. "What's the Colony?"

"A place for people who can't live in the City."

Valerie had never heard of people like that. The Foster Centre said there was only the City and the Outskirts, and the kids at the Centre could either be adopted into families or get their own place at eighteen. They hadn't told Valerie there was a third choice. Jack was the first person to show her she didn't have to follow the path set out by the Foster Centre. There could be another path. She stuffed the last bite of her sandwich in her mouth and washed it down with more water. "How much longer until we get there?"

"A couple hours."

Valerie scrunched up the sandwich wrapper and got up on unsteady legs. She willed herself to stand without help. There would be no one to help her soon. "And it's going to be my new home?"

Jack stood up and nodded. "I can't take you to live with me. My wife and I have a daughter and not enough money for a second child permit."

This was fine with Valerie. If she couldn't be with Henry, and her father didn't want her, she didn't want to be adopted, even by Jack. "Okay. Take me there; I want to see it."

…

Jack let Valerie sit on the passenger's seat for the last leg of their journey. There wasn't much to see, and the sunlight faded fast, but Valerie glued her eyes to the windshield. She couldn't remember leaving the City with her father, and she imagined she never had. It was her first trip south, and she wanted to soak up as much as she could.

On the trip, Jack answered her questions about where he lived – the Outskirts – and told Valerie a bit about his daughter Molly. He told Valerie about his smuggling runs that helped the Colony survive with food, medicines, clothing and household goods. However, when she asked about her father, all Jack would say is that her father would be in touch when it was safe. Valerie didn't like this answer or blame Jack for it. If her father had wanted her, she and Henry would be with him, safety or not. Jack wouldn't tell her either what danger her father was in. Valerie didn't care. Jack had come for her and was helping her, not her father.

She gasped when a wooden fence appeared in the distance. It stretched left and right farther than Valerie could see. She'd never seen anything made of wood before, with it being a rare and expensive material in the City. Jack steered the truck to a metal gate in the fence with a roofed wooden platform standing above it. He stopped the truck and reached for his seatbelt. "Stay here. I have to go unlatch the gate."

"I can do it." If she was going to live in this place, she wanted to know how to get in and out.

"It's a bit tricky. The latch is on the inside."

Valerie peered out the windshield, inspecting the gate illuminated in the truck's headlights. "I'll climb it."

Valerie was out the door and jogging to the gate before Jack could protest. She grabbed hold of the gate and pulled herself up and over it. On the other side, she slid her hands over it, until she found the latch. It was well-used and unlatched easily. The gate's hinges didn't creak as she opened it for Jack to drive in. He could've driven off and left her to find her own way, but he'd stayed, and he stopped the truck inside the gate, waiting for her to close it and get back in.

Valerie's father had faked his own death to get away from her and Henry, something she couldn't forgive him for. Jack, though, looked at her with what looked like pride when she got back in the car and fastened her seatbelt. Valerie didn't need her father, and as far as she was concerned, he could stay away forever.

Valerie leaned forward to gaze better out the windshield as Jack drove on, unable to see much with the headlights serving as the only illumination. "Is this the Colony?"

"Most of it is at the bottom of the slope. I'll take you to my contact's house where you can stay."

If Valerie couldn't live with Henry, she'd have to settle for Jack's contact. At least for now. The Foster Centre had taught her how to clean and do laundry, but they'd never instructed her in cooking. Not even when she was younger and still doing skills training with the goal of increasing desirability for potential families. Maybe they hadn't wanted her near sharp objects and sources of heat, with how much damage they could inflict.

"What're they like?" Valerie asked. If whomever it was insisted on treating her like a child, she'd need an exit plan.

"Jane is strong and self-reliant. I think you'll like her."

Valerie allowed herself a smile as they truck reached the slope and started down it, gaining speed as it went. Halfway down, she spotted two circles of small wooden huts, one smaller circle inside the other, larger one. Each house had lights shining through the windows, and people were in the street. This was where she was going to live. It seemed like a livelier place than the Foster Centre, and Valerie would have to find her place in it.

Jack drove up to one of the biggest houses in the inside circle and parked the truck. Valerie got out with her bag when he did and followed him to the door where he knocked.

A woman about Jack's age, with her hair tied back and wearing a t-shirt, flowy linen pants and strappy sandals opened the door. Valerie had never seen people dressed like that. In the Foster Centre, boots were the standard footwear as were thicker, formfitting pants.

The woman gave a warm smile. "You must be Valerie. Come in. I've been waiting for you."

Valerie was gaping and shut her mouth. Jack gestured for her to enter first, so she clutched her bag and strode inside, with Jack at her heels. "You knew I was coming?" Valerie hadn't known herself until that morning.

"Of course. The messenger Jack sent arrived yesterday."

"It wasn't a spontaneous event," Jack explained. "We spent months planning it, including where to bring you."

Months. While Valerie had scrubbed floors and dusted nooks and crannies, Jack had been planning how to rescue her. Valerie set her bag down and flung her arms around Jack, burying her face in his torso. "Thank you."

He returned the hug. It felt like what she imagined hugging her father would've been like if she'd grown up living with him. She lingered in the embrace, not wanting to stop the first bit of comfort she'd gotten since she was a little girl.

When Jack broke the hug, Valerie picked up her bag and held her chin high. "Thank you for taking me in," she said to Jane.

"You're welcome," Jane said. "Though you should know nothing in this place comes easy. You won't have free reign to do as you please without helping."

"I'll do whatever you need me to." Valerie meant it. There would be nothing worse than the other Colonists resenting her and thinking her useless. If she couldn't be with her brother, she had to be strong and brave for him.

Jane gave an approving nod. "Good. You can store your things in the first bedroom. We'll get you some new clothes when you're unpacked."

It didn't take long for Valerie to unpack her toiletries and the picture of her and Henry with their father that she kept for Henry's sake. She piled the clothes in her arms and walked back into the hallway where Jane and Jack waited. "What should I do with these?"

...

Jane took Valerie's old clothes to the Market in the centre of the Colony as a potential trade for some newer ones. The clothing vendor rummaged through the pile, barely glancing up at Jane or Valerie. "Yes, I can find use for these. You can take an equal amount in return."

It was the first time ever that Valerie had the freedom to choose her clothes. With Jane's guidance, she selected what was a nicer wardrobe than the Foster Centre pieces she'd handed the vendor.

Jane took Valerie's new clothes back to the house, leaving Jack to give Valerie a tour. The Colony didn't have much to it, just the Market in the middle surrounded by its own fence, the main fence with watch towers and the two rings of houses. Valerie's tour ended up being around the market, where Jack led her from vendor to vendor so she could find whatever she might need.

Between introductions, Jack told her the rules and the delivery schedule. All she had to do was report anyone unexpected approaching the fence if she was on watch tower duty, only take her allotted amount of goods, or extra acquired by trade, from the Market, and not harm other Colonists. The unspoken rule Valerie knew applied to her specifically was do whatever Jane requested. It wouldn't be difficult.

The vendors all lit up when Jack brought her around. They told Valerie stories of his help in difficult situations, or just because. His aid didn't come in terms of buying things or donating money, but in smuggling medicine and transporting people to the Colony. She saw the looks of awe and worship on their faces, of which Jack seemed oblivious. He was their hero, and more importantly, he was Valerie's.

Jack introduced her to other children her age, who were all there with their parents. There was little Valerie had in common with them, though she tried to relate.

At the end of the night, Valerie sat cross-legged on her bed and watched the sunrise through the small window. She was supposed to sleep now, in the heat of the day, but thoughts of Henry kept her awake. Jack was leaving at sundown, which meant Valerie would be alone with her thoughts and Jane. Was Henry happy with his foster parents? She hoped so. Did he remember her? She didn't know. He'd been so young when they took him from her.

Unable to calm her mind, Valerie exited her room, crept through the small house and stepped outside. The hot air hit her skin, forming beads of sweat, which she let drip. She turned the corner of the building and crouched. In the dirt, she wrote Henry's name and rested her palm on top. Even if he never remembered her or saw her again, she'd keep her brother alive in her mind. And if there were more kids that came to the Colony with no one, she would help them. That was the only way she could honour her brother now.

The Courtship Agreement

Ben

Ben didn't take his eyes off his plate as he ate supper with his parents. That didn't mean he wasn't listening and observing. His father, Bob, was grumbling about his soon-to-be increased workload once Clinic Day rolled around and he had Courtship applications to go through. He was, of course, professional and non-biased while performing his duties, at least to the extent required by law.

Ben's mother, Annette, was hardly paying attention to her husband's complaints, having grown used to hearing them every year. In truth, Bob loved his work and the power it gave him. He complained only because he needed to have something to complain about so it didn't appear he was too attached.

Ben had higher ambitions for himself than being the Courtship Reviewer. He wanted to be the City's Leader. The first step on that path was moving out of his parents' house, but for that he had to either wait until he was eighteen or in a Courtship. Ben would've waited the year until his eighteenth birthday, except he needed a Courtship for influential people to see him as serious and successful.

He'd finally found the perfect candidate. Not perfect as in attractive. *No.* It didn't hurt that the boy he'd chosen was good looking, but Ben had attraction towards no one. Love and romance were meaningless. He didn't believe that those concepts made anyone happy. Only money, power and influence could do that, no matter what the old cliché said. His parents had married to improve their own positions in the Government, having come from lower-level working families. It had worked out for them, and Ben hoped to replicate, if not better, it.

His perfect Courtship candidate was an easy to control foster kid living with a couple that didn't want him. He had no knowledge of his birth family, though Ben had ideas of whom his father was. It was a rumour that Malcolm Connor, one of Bob's coworkers in the Government, had children he'd given up when joining the Government. Ben didn't know what happened to the second child. He'd only tracked down Henry. It was a perfect piece of leverage over Malcolm that Ben could keep for when the time was right, if he needed Henry for that long. He had no intentions of ever telling Henry about his father.

The dilemma Ben had was choosing the most opportune time to announce his choice. His father would automatically grant the Courtship, which was a major perk of being the Reviewer's son, but it still had to look legit, should anyone dare to question it.

When Bob ceased his complaints about work, and Annette took a sip of her water, Ben set down his fork, lifted his head and cleared his throat. That was enough to get the attention of his parents.

When they were both looking at him, Ben spoke. "I've decided to apply for a Courtship this year."

"That's wonderful, dear," Annette said as she placed her hand on his.

Bob leaned back in his chair. "I trust you've chosen your Courtship Partner wisely."

Ben could feel a wicked grin grow on his face, and he didn't try to stop it. Why should he? He was finally making progress towards the life he envisioned. "Yes."

That was all his parents had to say on the matter, which might've bothered other people. It didn't bother Ben. His parents wanted him to have ambition. They'd raised him to be smart, calculating and confident, and they trusted his judgement. He liked the freedom they afforded him to make decisions.

If he'd been the partying type, he would've taken advantage of his parents' positions to get out of fines for breaking the curfew. He'd tested that limit a couple times, and he and his parents had never had to pay a single coin. Knowing he could get away with it was enough, and he'd never enjoyed staying out late with nothing to do, so he stopped doing it.

He did take advantage of their money to get himself a car the moment he was old enough to drive one. Someone else cleaned it, but Ben was a careful driver. Getting dents out only took time he didn't want to spend waiting. With his parents at work as often as they were, going without his personal car would mean hiring out a driver, walking or, worse, taking the bus. That was a low Ben wouldn't stoop to.

The afternoon after telling his parents his intentions, Ben combed his black hair, put on a button-down shirt and a pair of trousers, and went outside to his car to drive to the Newsomes' address. They had an idea he was coming and had sent Henry out. It didn't matter where. Later, Ben would approach Henry and make him think he was getting a proposal not engineered in advance. Right now, he had a deal to make. It was better not to have Henry around for that.

While Ben's parents lived in a house in the rich Quarters, the Newsomes lived in an Apartment District. Normally, Ben would never venture into those. However, this was a necessity. He kept his eyes on the road and tried not to cringe at the deprivation around him as he drove south. Surely Henry would be grateful to Ben for rescuing him from this situation, though Ben had an inkling that he would end up in an apartment for at least a few years. His parents had done so in their Courtship and the early years of their marriage, only moving into their house when their finances had allowed. That was all before Ben had been born. There was no shame in living in a penthouse, he knew, especially in Apartment District 1 or 2. Any farther south would be too deprived. He needed some sense of civility.

It was easy to find a parking space in front of the Newsomes' building with the lack of cars this far south. Ben's was the only vehicle parked along their street. He locked it and shrugged before going inside, riding the elevator to their floor and knocking on their door.

A large man with a stern face, who had to be Reginald, opened the door. Behind him stood his wife Eleanor. Reginald swept his hand, gesturing for Ben to enter.

It was a modest, two-bedroom apartment, though they had the means to have a phone installed. It sat on a table in their living room near the wall screen. Ben's parents had no power over news broadcasts, so he could only hope luck was on his side and the screen wouldn't come on.

"Henry isn't here, is he?" Ben asked as he stepped into the living room with the Newsomes. At least their couch wasn't terribly uncomfortable when he sat on it.

"No," Eleanor said. "He went out with his friend. We didn't even need to persuade him."

Ben's ears prickled at the mention of his friend. That was a matter he would quash later. Henry needed to focus solely on Ben for the arrangement to work in Ben's favour. For now, he ignored the matter. "Good."

"No offence," Reginald said, "but it is hard to believe anyone wants to marry Henry."

Ben didn't intend to marry Henry. That was a bond that potentially would be too expensive for him to break. Tying himself down forever wasn't the aim, nor was going through the arduous process of a divorce. Those were harder to get than Courtships. Projecting an image was, and for that he needed a Courtship. "He's exactly what I'm looking for," he told the Newsomes with his most-charming smile, the one reserved for getting his way. "And it'll get him out of your hair. It's a win for all parties."

Eleanor crossed her arms over her torso and snorted. "You'll never get him to agree to such a transaction. He has ideas in his head of finding someone who loves him."

Ben didn't know where Henry had gotten such a notion. His foster parents clearly didn't have love for him, nor did Malcolm. Perhaps the lack of it made him want it more. It was an idea Ben felt was foolish and a waste of time. He wasn't about to give Henry actual love, yet he could pretend, or create the illusion of it, long enough to get to Clinic Day. Surely, it couldn't be that difficult. "I don't plan on telling him about this. He'll think he's getting a genuine proposal."

That was enough to satisfy the Newsomes, and they got down to the business end of their meeting. It was true that most Courtship applicants let their emotions guide their decisions, and many of them got rejections. The desperate ones, who would marry anyone to avoid being alone, got mixed results, often going through the review process. Ben would take neither of those paths.

In previous times, long before the City existed, there had often been dowry payments, or some form of money exchanged, as part of marriage negotiations. It wasn't common now that most people were too poor to have expendable income, but Ben had plenty, and the Newsomes were bitter about paying the Foster Centre for Henry when he'd been such a massive disappointment. Their version of a disappointment and failure was exactly what Ben needed. It would make Henry easy to control and influence, and when the time came to dissolve the Courtship, Henry wouldn't be able to do anything about it.

After some back and forth, Ben and the Newsomes agreed on a sum a margin over what they'd paid the Foster Centre to account for the years they'd housed him. Ben handed over half, with the understanding of paying the other half when he had a Courtship acceptance.

Ben didn't ask for details on Henry's likes and dislikes. Whatever they were, they wouldn't prevent Ben from getting his Courtship. The few details the Newsomes had told him, in this and their prior conversation, made Henry appear like a timid, spineless, boy desperate for approval. Ben could work with that.

With the discussion done and the agreement settled, Ben left the Newsomes' apartment. He had planning to do. It was customary to give a token while proposing, derived from the times before the City when engagement rings were the norm. That was before the gem supply consisted of repurposed ones from surrendered jewelry as payment for fines. Now, only those wealthy enough to buy jewelry, or lucky enough to inherit some, gave it as their token. Ben could afford it if he'd wanted to, except he didn't intend on spending much money on Henry. This wasn't a love match.

He needed something disposable and not overly expensive, but something that would still impress Henry. A few ideas bounced through his brain over the coming days, and he dismissed them as impractical or just not good enough. It was when he was in the market with his father, getting their weekly rations, plus extras paid for out of pocket because they could, that Ben found the perfect item.

In the rich Quarters, markets had entire aisles of confections. The people shopping in them had enough money to afford those kinds of indulgences. They weren't things the Newsomes would've bought Henry. He sent his father on ahead and strode down the aisle. Many of the confections were bright, colourful candies, which seemed too childish. Yet, amidst the garish candies meant to attract children, were bars and boxes of chocolate. This was perfect. Something sweet yet refined.

Ben selected a solid bar of chocolate and a box of filled and decorated chocolates. The box was what he'd give Henry during the proposal. He'd keep the bar for later.

When he'd finished helping his father shop, and paid for his chocolates, Ben diverted his thoughts to the small details of the proposal. He certainly wasn't going to do it at the Newsomes' apartment, or at his house. That left Henry's school or getting Henry to meet him somewhere else. The latter choice was preferable. Ben had no desire to mingle with the City's poorest in front of the Apartment District high school again. Doing that might even let Henry's friend add their opinion, and Ben would not accept anything less than a yes from Henry.

When Ben had arranged to meet Henry, he'd gone to wait for him outside the Apartment District school, and to Ben's relief, Henry had exited the building alone. Ben had felt like a predator hunting the most willing and oblivious prey that day. All it had taken was a charming smile and some generic compliments to get Henry to walk to the bus stop with him.

It hadn't been that easy since. Henry had often been in the company of another boy his age, who must've been the friend the Newsomes mentioned, which made it harder for Ben to get Henry alone. After some investigating, based on the name Henry had unwittingly supplied him, Ben and deduced that this was Carl Wessin's orphan ward. It wasn't hard to figure that out once he'd paid for the Foster Centre records of boys named Gavriel that were around Henry's age.

It was an interesting development, and a nice piece of Ben's plan. The way to control Henry lay with Gavriel, who was a threat to Ben's ambitions. He wasn't about to let a foster kid steal the position that was rightfully his.

Ben almost felt bad for the girl whom Gavriel had attached himself too. She was a bystander Ben had no grievances with, and she was unimportant. It almost made him change his mind about having her and Gavriel's inevitable Courtship application declined, after a fake review, but he couldn't let Gavriel make steps towards things that were Ben's. That mess was the following year's problem as the girl was only fifteen.

For now, he needed to hook Henry. To that end, he sent Henry a note in the mail requesting a meeting at one of the parks in Quarter 1. It was free, but it should've impressed Henry. Greenery of any kind was sparse in the Apartment Districts, and the few green spaces they had were basic and unimpressive patches of grass and scraggly bushes in crowded areas. None of those would do.

On the day he'd decided upon, Ben dressed in a blue sport coat with khaki pants and brushed his black hair back. The harsh colour of his hair always made his skin seem paler than it already was, and there was no helping it. He didn't tan, or have the desire too, nor did he want to bleach his hair. It didn't matter. He wasn't trying to be attractive to Henry, though that would help his plans.

He set out with plenty of time, preferring to arrive early and watch Henry walk up. When he parked his car and entered the park, he walked to a bench with a clear view of the gate and unimpeded from the path, and he sat with his legs crossed at the ankle and his hands resting on the bench.

The sun was out in the blue sky, and there was a gentle breeze. It had been a while since the last rainfall, so the greenery had to be watered with sprinklers. In the Apartment Districts, plants withered from lack of water, but not here. The City's wealthy liked to look at bright, blooming flowers and lush, green grass. Ben wasn't a nature enthusiast, yet even he preferred the park's look to that of dead and dried up plants.

Ben kept one eye on the entrance while he looked around. There were plenty of families there leading their kids to the playground. Many of the families had two children, but more than a few had only one, which was the limit before buying a second child permit.

If Ben had a child in his plans, he would stop at only one. His parents had never bought a second child permit, preferring to spend their money on other things. Malcolm Connor had obviously bought two child permits, and that had turned out so poorly for him that he'd lost both children and had no spouse Ben knew of. As far as Ben knew, Malcolm really didn't contact either of his children. Perhaps he'd gladly traded them for his privileged job and the power that came with it. Whatever the reason, it wouldn't stop Ben from thinking about how to use Henry against Malcolm. He would wait for the right opportunity. To use his leverage too early would be a waste.

His decided upon meeting time approached, and Ben grew impatient. He was almost ready to leave and give the Newsomes an unhappy phone call, when Henry finally walked in.

His outfit of a jacket, shirt and pants was nothing spectacular, but Ben doubted the Newsomes bought him high quality clothes. The jacket seemed a size or two too big as the sleeves were baggy, and he hadn't fastened the front. Ben was going to have to buy Henry new clothes. Otherwise, he'd worsen Ben's image, which would never do.

Henry walked with a hunch to his shoulders, like he was trying to fade into the background without drawing anyone's attention. He had Ben's, though he didn't appear to see Ben.

Ben rose from the bench, brushed off his sport coat and strode in Henry's direction, keeping his pace casual. "You came. I wasn't sure you would."

Henry hung his head and slouched his shoulders even more. Ben hadn't tried to accuse Henry of anything, and here he was acting ashamed.

Henry took a ragged breath. "I'm sorry I'm late."

Ben expected to hear a reason why, or an excuse, but Henry made none. So, Ben shrugged and offered Henry his hand. "You're fine. Walk with me?"

It was more of a demand than a request, and Henry seemed to understand that. He accepted Ben's hand, risking a minor violation of the affection laws, and Ben led him father into the garden. When they came to a fork, he steered Henry on the path heading away from the playground and the noise of children.

"I hope this isn't too tame of a date for you," Ben said when they reached a mostly secluded section of the park with trees and shrubbery that supplied a modicum of privacy. He dropped Henry's hand and took a step away to see him clearer.

Henry's cheeks flushed pink, and he blinked. "It isn't, but I don't understand why you'd ask me on a date."

His lack of self confidence and self esteem only made Ben more certain he'd chosen the right Courtship partner. Henry was desperate for reassurance;

Ben only needed to give him a little bit, and he'd have Henry under his control. "You don't realize your own attractiveness? Such a shame."

It wasn't a lie that Henry was good looking, even to Ben.

"Heh," Henry chuckled, his blush deepening, and he met Ben's eyes. "I suppose I don't, but I do realize yours."

Ben didn't particularly care whether Henry found him attractive, though it did help his cause, so he ran with it. He stepped closer to Henry, maintaining eye contact as he went. "Do you?" he asked with an arched eyebrow when his mouth was within centimetres of Henry's.

Henry gave a single nod.

"Sounds like we should act on it." There was no one around to see as he put his hands on Henry's waist and gave a tug, bringing Henry closer. That was a good thing. Although he could've afforded to pay a fine for breaking the public affection law for people outside of Courtships and marriages, he didn't want to. This was a bit of acting he didn't want an audience for.

Henry, for his part, lifted his arms and crossed his wrists behind Ben's neck.

Ben titled his head to the side and brought his lips to Henry's. Where other people might've felt weak in the knees or like the world was spinning, Ben felt nothing. His kissing skills weren't superb, but they were enough to deepen the blush on Henry's face, dilate his pupils when he opened his eyes and summon a shy grin to his face.

Ben he would need to do this again, just to continue the charade of feeling anything for Henry that was necessary to prolong their Courtship. It was a role he would fulfill if it furthered his aims.

Ben's hand went to the box of chocolates in his sport coat pocket. There wasn't going to be a better opportunity to spring his proposal. He looked at

Henry and forced himself to wear a relaxed smile. "I have a question for you."

Henry was standing with less of a hunch now. It was amazing what boost he'd gotten from a single kiss. It had likely been the most affection he'd had since Malcolm abandoned him. Ben almost pitied him. "Alright."

Ben pulled out the box of chocolates and presented it to Henry. "Will you get a Courtship with me?"

Henry's lips parted and his eyebrows went up. "You want to marry me? We hardly know each other."

Ben hadn't expected to get a straightforward yes from Henry. It would take some convincing. "I know enough to know I don't want to wait another year, and I don't believe you want to live with the Newsomes that much longer."

A flash of hurt and anger went through Henry's eyes at the mention of his foster parents, as Ben had expected. He pressed on. "I promise you'll like living with me more. This is your chance to get away from them."

Henry hesitated, clearly tempted by this. "I don't want to marry someone unless they love me."

After Eleanor's remark that Henry had this idealistic notion, Ben had a lie prepared for it. "With time, I'm sure love can grow between us. It won't be instant. You just need to take a chance."

Ben saw Henry gulp, followed by resolve settling on his face and he took the box of chocolates. "Alright. I'll apply for a Courtship with you."

Ben spent the rest of the afternoon with Henry. They sat on a bench with the box of chocolates, which Ben only accepted one piece of. He let Henry have the rest, insisted on it even, and he didn't have to fake his gleeful smile. The first step in his plan to power was complete, and it hadn't taken too much effort. Whether future steps would require more effort was yet to be seen, but

Ben had practice at showing people what they wanted. It had worked on his teachers and his parents, so there was no reason it wouldn't work on Henry for as long as Ben needed it to.

Between the chocolates, Ben gave vague details about his parents, and listened to Henry bemoan his living arrangement with the Newsomes. Ben played at being sympathetic, going so far as to rest his hand on Henry's. Acting like he was a better choice of person to live with than Henry's foster parents was key to keeping Henry on board with getting a Courtship. That was all that mattered to Ben, and he'd act however and say whatever he needed to reach that goal.

To further his performance of a doting intended Courtship partner, when it was time to leave, Ben insisted on driving Henry home. Pretending to care, and taking Henry's side, would be key in the lead up to Clinic Day. It was a small price to pay for the advantage Ben had earned himself.

He couldn't stop himself from grinning from the endorphin rush victory gave him as he walked into his parents' house and kicked off his shoes before going to his father's home office to deliver the news. Finally, he was on his way to the life he had planned. The fact that Henry was a disposable pawn in it made no difference at all.

The Devout

Sage

Sage climbed the staircase in her apartment building. Most people living on her floor took the elevator, but Sage had decided to skip it instead of waiting in the lobby for it to make its slow descent. One glance at the tracker to see it was on the sixteenth floor told her the wait would be long, so she put one foot in front of the other and hauled herself up and up to her floor.

Her legs were wobbly and weak by the time she reached her apartment, got inside and collapsed on her bed. All she could do was pant and raise one arm to swipe at the sweat on her forehead. It wouldn't be long before her parents came home and she had to get up to help make supper. At least she had a few minutes before that.

It gave Sage time to rehearse what she would say when her mom inevitably brought up the idea of her applying for a Courtship again. In a way, she was glad that her parents were friends with Ethan and Kelsie Alexander. That had let Sage become friendly with their son Max, but it didn't mean she wanted to marry him. He was three years older, had ties to the Rebel Cause and was so serious.

Sage's parents were members of the Devout, an organization loyal to the Government and lining its own pockets. That was how they lived in Apartment District 2 on one of the higher floors of their building. Sage's parents had raised her to be a faithful member, which was another reason she didn't understand why they pushed Max so hard on her.

"Sage Parker, what are you doing?"

Sage's mom, Kylie, stood in Sage's bedroom doorway with her hands planted on her hips and fire in her eyes that deepened the red of her hair.

Sage pushed herself up with her elbows. She hadn't heard her mom come in the apartment. Perhaps she'd been in the room she shared with Sage's dad Lucas, and Sage hadn't beaten them home. "Trying to catch my breath. I'll come help with supper in a minute."

Kylie huffed, stepped into Sage's room and opened the closet door. She rustled through the rack of clothes until she found what she was looking for.

Sage sighed upon seeing the forest green dress in her mom's arms. That dress meant one of two things: her parents were taking her out to eat, or they'd set her up on a date with Max.

Kylie held the dress out to Sage, waiting for her to take it. "Get dressed, put on some makeup, and do try to tame your hair."

When her mom was gone, Sage got to her feet with a groan. First, she shut her door. Then she stood in front of her bed and stared at the dress. She was always more comfortable in pants and boots, not dresses and heels. When she'd been little, her parents had dressed her in frills just because they could afford to. Once she'd gotten old enough to have an opinion and impose it, they'd back off on dressing her like a doll. At least on a daily basis.

Thirty minutes later, Sage stepped out of her room. Her red hair was up in pins, and she'd applied makeup for the first time in weeks. The worst part of her ensemble was her heels. Every step she took was wobbly.

Her dad was in the living room dressed in a tailored suit. At least that answered Sage's question as to why her mom had made her dress up.

Lucas gave her a once over, surprise lighting in his eyes. "That was fast. You're sure you're ready?"

"Mm-hmm, but I can go sit in my room and pretend to need more time."

Lucas snorted.

"Where are we going?" Sage asked.

"A business meeting. We're trying to expand our range of goods."

Sage held back her eyeroll. Her parents used to leave her home for those, and the few she'd gone to were dull affairs. "I wish mom had arranged a date for me and Max instead. At least he's not boring."

Lucas's eyes bored into Sage with an intensity that made her tense up. "There's no point in that if you're not going to apply for a Courtship with him. You're hardly a child anymore, Sage."

"We don't like each other that way." Sage and Max wouldn't make a good match for a marriage when they disagreed on so many things. She'd assumed that they could at least have a friendship, or acquaintance. Perhaps they couldn't now that Sage was old enough for the dating laws to apply to her.

"A fact I'm glad for," Lucas said. "Your mom is too sentimental when it comes to the Alexanders."

For as long as Sage could remember, her mom had only spoken fondly of Ethan Alexander, Max's dad. Kylie was even close to Max's mom Kelsie. Sage hadn't thought too much about her own dad's views, had only assumed that the friendship extended to both of her parents. Before she could ask about Lucas's remarks, Kylie came into the living room wearing her best dress, jewelry, makeup and her hair up in pins.

Kylie was glamorous while Sage like a dressed-up doll. It didn't help that they shared the same fiery red hair. On Kylie it was vivacious, while on Sage it looked like a too-vivid wig. Sage would've preferred to inherit her dad's blonde hair, but she hadn't been that lucky.

Kylie strode past Sage and Lucas and reached for the doorknob. "We're going to be late."

This time Sage rolled her eyes. It was just like her mom to be the last one ready and then rush Sage and Lucas.

Her parents stood side-by-side in the elevator, Kylie's hand resting on Lucas's arm. They were experts at presenting a united front, and Sage knew it wasn't all an act. There was genuine love between them, the kind Kylie wanted Sage to have for Max.

Sage didn't like anyone enough to apply for a Courtship and saw no point in rushing into one. She had her friends Peter and Evelyn, though she was often the third wheel of their group. If any couple should've gotten a Courtship, it was Peter and Evelyn, yet they seemed in no rush. That suited Sage; if they did get married, they'd have no time for her.

When the elevator reached the lobby, Sage followed her parents outside to a waiting car. Her parents didn't own their own car. They could've afforded to, but there were few spaces to park one outside their apartment building. It was assumed that anyone who lived in an Apartment District rode the bus or walked. The Parkers normally took the bus, and they hired out a car for business and Devout functions.

Sage liked having a hired chauffer. It made her feel wealthier than she was, and it was magnitudes better than riding a cramped bus.

That day's destination was a high-rise office building in Apartment District 1. Sage stepped out of the car and followed her parents across the small parking lot to the main door.

Kylie turned to Sage and adjusted some of the pins in her hair and tucked in loose strands. "Remember to be on your best behaviour. It's vital that this meeting goes well."

Lucas opened the door and held it for Sage and Kylie, only walking through once they were inside. "We need to make a favourable impression."

"I know how to act in public," Sage said. If they were convinced that she was a liability, they could've left her at home. She wasn't that invested in proving her worth during a stuffy and boring meeting.

"A reminder never hurts," Kylie said. She turned away from Sage and walked arm-in-arm with Lucas to the elevator call button.

Sage scurried after her parents. They didn't need to tell her with words to follow. If they'd brought her to leave her in the lobby, they would've left her at home.

The elevator rose to a floor higher than the top storey of their apartment building. When it finally opened, Sage guessed they were about two-thirds up the building. Whomever they were meeting was important, but not *that* important, which was just the type that her parents liked to work with.

Sage trailed her parents down the white hallway to a set of double doors. One side was open, revealing a large office that had to take up an eighth of the floor. Her eyebrows shot up. If someone on this floor needed such a large space, how massive were the offices on the top floor?

The inside of the office had a carved stone desk in front of a wingback armchair with burgundy cushions backed against the large window. Shelves of books covered the entire lefthand wall, and the space across from the desk, just inside the doors, had smaller chairs with the same burgundy upholstery and a stone coffee table with glass top. A plush rug in a deep grey hue covered most of the floor, only leaving the edges of the room bare. It was altogether too much, not even considering the small statues and the framed artwork on the righthand wall.

A gilded plaque on the closed side of the door read: Mr. S. Kolvey. Sage peered at the name, wondering what the S might stand for. Whatever his first name was, Mr. Kolvey wasn't in his office. Obviously, he was one of those self-important people who wasted other people's time.

While Sage examined the décor, her parents strode into the office. "Are you certain about this, Luc?" Sage heard her mom whisper.

It was an interesting question that made Sage's ears perk up. Her parents usually portrayed such a united front. She assumed they agreed on everything.

"You know we have little choice. It's too late for doubts."

Kylie nodded and squared her shoulders. She seemed to notice Sage hadn't walked in with her and Lucas and called over her shoulder. "Sage, stop gawking in the hall."

Kylie had to be on edge to be barking at Sage in public. Still, Sage knew better than to argue with her mom when Mr. Kolvey could show up at any moment, so she walked in and stood next to her parents.

Sage had no knowledge of what this meeting was about; she only knew it had her parents at odds. Perhaps Mr. Kolvey would provide some clarity.

He strode into his office and shook Lucas's hand then Kylie's. While he greeted her parents, Sage sized him up. He wore an immaculate suit with gold cufflinks and a satin tie, and his shoes shined so intensely Sage's eyes hurt from looking at them. His dark hair was cut short and styled with a side part.

"You must be Sage," he said, offering her his hand when he was finished with her parents.

Sage grasped his hand and shook it, keeping her grip firm while making eye contact. Lucas had taught her the importance of that. "I am."

Mr. Kolvey grinned wide. "I see you have your mother's fashion sense."

Sage wasn't about to tell him that Kylie had picked out her entire outfit from the store. Correcting the man her parents wanted to do business with was a poor move. "I suppose I do."

Kylie patted Sage on the shoulder and smiled. "Have you thought about our proposal, Mr. Kolvey?"

Mr. Kolvey sat on one of the chairs and gestured for Sage and her parents to do the same. "Straight to business, I see."

When everyone was seated, he reclined, rested his elbows on his knees, and tented his fingers. "I must confess, Mrs. Parker, I have my reservations about having my wares sent to the Colony with no oversight. How are we to be sure the Rebels aren't selling them on the black market for profit?"

Kylie glanced at Lucas, who nodded. "The Devout have had ties to the Rebel Cause since its inception." She meant Max's parents. "But I understand your concerns, Mr. Kolvey. We've decided to install Sage as an officer to report on the Rebel's delivery driver and audit the cargo."

As the statement left Kylie's mouth, she and Lucas turned to Sage. She blinked. It hadn't occurred to her that her parents would use her as leverage to cement a deal, nor had they told her of this before hand. They must've set their sights on a large profit from whatever his wares were.

"I wouldn't normally trust a sixteen-year-old with such a task," Mr. Kolvey said. "Though one raised in loyalty to the Government could be worth taking a chance on."

"I would never side with the Rebels, Mr. Kolvey." Sage kept her posture erect and her eyes on him. Even though her parents hadn't briefed her on this, she wasn't afraid. A larger role in the Devout was what she wanted, so she could decide whether she wanted to be a member. Until then, her ties to it were through her parents. "It isn't disloyal to the Government to help troublemakers leave the City. That can only help the overpopulation problem and save money in the prison."

Mr. Kolvey sat up, seeming pleased with Sage's remarks. "I'll consent to a trial agreement. If things go well after a few months, we can discuss a more permanent arrangement."

Sage sat back as her parents finalized their deal with Mr. Kolvey. At sixteen, with no Courtship, her signature had no authority on contracts, so she left that to her parents.

The meeting and Sage's new role weren't things Sage and her parents could discuss in the elevator or in their hired car. Sage had to wait until they got home. That was normally where they went after meetings. However, this time Lucas directed the car to a restaurant. Mr. Kolvey's deal had to be lucrative for her parents to splurge on a meal in a fancy eatery.

Kylie pulled out a compact mirror to assess her face and hair. When she was finished primping, she handed it to Sage with a tube of lipstick.

Sage accepted and opened both. On most days, she left her face and lips bare, but a glance at the other patrons going inside with their best clothes and jewels on told her she had to look immaculate. Even with re-applied lipstick and flyaway strands of hair tucked into pins, Sage felt underdressed. Her parents weren't wealthy enough to afford jewelry, besides the necklace Lucas had given Kylie for a proposal gift and their wedding rings. Even those seemed cheap compared to the jewels on the necks, wrists and ears of diners around them. That didn't deter her parents from strutting to the door with their heads high.

Sage followed, trying to emulate her mom's confidence. The last thing she needed was to be the reason why the maitre d' refused them entry.

Lucas told the maitre d' his name, and the man scanned the list before crossing off an entry. He tucked three menus under his arm and gestured into the restaurant. "This way please."

Sage had to work hard not to gawk at the opulence of the interior. There were white linen tablecloths on the tables, set with crystal glasses, polished cutlery and intricately folded napkins tucked into rings. The walls were a deep burgundy with gold accents, and framed paintings hung between potted plants. Even the mirrored floor and cathedral ceiling were fancier than Sage was accustomed to. She saw now why her mom had instructed her to dress up. It wasn't for Mr. Kolvey's benefit. It was for this.

When they reached their table, Lucas pulled out Kylie's chair while the maitre d' pulled Sage's before placing the menus on the table. When Sage sat, the man pushed her chair in. "Your server will be with you momentarily."

Her parents picked up their menu and flipped open the covers, and Sage left hers untouched for the time being. "Why are we here?" she asked, having the sense to keep her voice down.

Her dad set his menu down and gazed at her, while Kylie simply closed hers and kept a hold on it. "This is an example of what you can have, Sage, if our deal with Mr. Kolvey goes well," Lucas said.

"It's a treat for now, like a premature reward for the part you'll play," Kylie said.

Sage wrung her hands on her lap, glad the table obscured it from her parents. "I've always wanted to do my part, though this seems sudden." There had never been suspicion worth warranting from the Devout about what the Rebel Cause did with the goods they bought. Why had that changed?

"It's been coming since the Rebels got a new driver," Lucas said. "We've kept an eye on him, and now it's time to act. You shouldn't worry, Sage. We would never put you in harm's way."

Kylie reached over and rested her hand on Sage's arm. "The job is straightforward. There's nothing to worry about."

Sage hadn't been worried. The Devout had Government protection, unlike the Rebel Cause. What Max and his parents did had always seemed more dangerous to her, especially since he'd joined the Guard Corps.

"Won't the Rebels be upset about us checking up on them?" Sage asked as she grabbed her menu.

Kylie flicked her hand in a dismissive gesture. "Their feelings are irrelevant. Besides, you chose your side when you turned down Max."

Max. Sage wondered whether he'd be disappointed in her for doing this job for her parents. It shouldn't have mattered, considering there was nothing between them, yet it still felt like something she should tell him.

The waiter came before Sage could form a coherent response to her mom's statement. Sage let her parents order first while she scanned the menu. When it was her turn, she ordered the last item her eyes landed on: a mushroom fettucine dish. It wasn't the worst decision she could've made, though Sage wasn't a mushroom fanatic. They were normally too earthy for her, but the dish, when it came, was subtle.

Sage's mind wandered to Max as she ate and rode home with her parents. When she was back in her bedroom, she pulled out a note pad and scrawled him a note, folding the paper and sealing it with tape when she was finished so she could write out his address on the black side. Her parents could've afforded envelopes, and would've bought them, if the Government hadn't limited their suppl in the name of preserving paper. Mailed notes were the most common form of communication in the City with few people being able to afford phones, and even with mandatory recycling, people still tucked letters and notes away as mementos, and the recycling plant could only work so fast. So almost everyone folded up and sealed their correspondences and wrote addresses on the back. It made Sage feel common, like she could be anyone.

Barely a day passed since she mailed it when Max's response came. Sage entered her apartment after school to find a note on her bed with his handwriting. She tore it open, read his short reply, and darted from her room to pull her boots on and grab the elevator, calling out to her parents to tell them she was going out as she went out the door.

Sage didn't need a bus to go to her meeting place with Max. It was always faster to go on foot, especially when she ran.

Max was waiting outside the café when Sage arrived. He was wearing street clothes, not his guard uniform. Sage supposed it would've been weird, not to mention against Guard policy, for him to meet her while on duty.

He held the door for Sage and entered the café behind her. Once they ordered pastries and drinks and grabbed a table in the back corner, Max fixed his eyes on Sage. "What's this about? Your note sounded urgent."

Sage took a sip of her lemonade and set the glass down with a thump. She told him the shortened version of her parents' meeting with Mr. Kolvey and her new role. "It felt like a betrayal not to tell you."

Max heaved a sigh. "We're on different sides, Sage. Your mom has history with my dad, which is the only thing making us not enemies. You don't need to protect me."

Sage arched an eyebrow. "You don't care that I'll be reporting on your organisation?" Perhaps she'd assumed wrongly that Max would appreciate the heads-up. Maybe there couldn't be friendship between them, and she'd blown her only chance at it when she'd decided not to marry him.

He smiled. "I appreciate you telling me, but it's not a surprise. Your parents trusted Jack because they knew him. Of course they're going to watch Charlie and have suspicions."

Sage's mind spun with the fragments of an idea. Perhaps her new role could benefit Max as well. "Maybe we can both get something out of this." She met his eyes, trying to make her meaning clear. "I could give you intel in return. Our friendship doesn't have to end, Max. If our parents worked together, so can we as long as we have common interests."

Max pursed his lips, considering. When he seemed to come to a decision, he nodded. "It could work for now if we're careful. A lot of our members and yours will be furious if they find out."

Sage donned a cheeky grin. "I'm not so naïve as to go making it obvious. You can grant me more credit than that."

"Oh, I know. I would never dare underestimate you."

Later, when Sage was back in her bedroom, she collapsed onto her bed with a smile on her face. Making a deal with Max was the right thing to do. The Devout were noble, but the Rebel Cause had its usefulness too. If they started making trouble, and affecting Devout business, the deal she'd made would dissolve, and Sage would choose her side. It wasn't tied to marrying or not marrying anyone, like her parents believed. What side Sage fell on would be a personal decision she would make when she had to. In the meantime, she would act like the loyal Devout member her parents expected.

Her first task would be going to meet Charlie for the first time. She knew little about him, only a few details she dragged out of Max. Charlie was in his twenties, lived alone and had no living family. That had made him a perfect candidate, in the Rebel Cause's view, for replacing Jack Birch as their Colony delivery driver. It wasn't much for Sage, which was fine as she didn't need to know intimate details on his life to report on him.

That gave her confidence on the day her parents sent her to meet him. There would be no training period. From the first time, The Devout expected Sage to write a report.

Sage stuck her clipboard, a pen and some paper into a backpack and headed out for the bus. When it arrived at her stop in Apartment District 8, she shuddered at the deprivation and dirt everywhere. She willed herself not to see it as she walked to the place Charlie would be. The first impression he got couldn't be of her rattled.

The first impression she gave him, regardless of her intentions, was one of a young girl out of her element. As soon as Sage caught a glimpse of him, she stopped and stumbled, her jaw dropping open.

Charlie was leaning against the side of a pickup truck with faded paint parked at the edge of the dusty road next to a crumbling building. He had his legs crossed at the ankle and his hands stuffed into the pockets of his dark pants. Plastic crates and canvas sacks covered the bed of the truck, showing that he was either leaving for a delivery or finishing one. Either way, he looked like he was expecting her.

The scene was something foreign to Sage, having only joined her parents for negotiations with wealthy businesspeople. She'd never seen what happened once the Rebel Cause got hold of goods, and even this was just a taste.

He gave Sage a smirk while she was still gawking at the scene. Of course the meeting place was on the most abandoned and dirty street in the Apartment District.

"You're the girl they sent to check up on me," Charlie said in a relaxed drawl. "This'll be interesting."

Choosing a Side

Gavriel

Gavriel sat on the thin mattress atop a metal bed bolted to the floor. The entire room was covered in rivetted sheets of metal, including the back of the door and every piece of the attached bathroom, and there was no window or mirror. The bed was the only piece of furniture.

One moment he'd been trailing Molly on foot in the middle of nowhere under a dark sky. Watching where to step had taken all his focus. He was so unobservant that he hadn't known anyone was lurking in the shadows until a man clamped a hand over his mouth and carted him off like a sack of potatoes. Gavriel couldn't have made a sound, though he heard a girl's shout of 'run!' and responding footsteps.

The man had carried him a fair distance in the opposite direction from the one Molly had gone and thrown him into a car's backseat. Gavriel had landed hard on his side with a grunt. As he'd sat up, he'd seen one man at the wheel and another sitting beside Gavriel. They'd been burly men, wearing black clothes, shoes and hats.

"You messed up bad," the one sitting beside Gavriel had growled as the car had taken off.

Gavriel hadn't understood why they'd taken him or where, and he still didn't. The men had ignored his questions as they'd driven non-stop until they reached a tower on the City's north coast and dragged him across shifting, grainy ground and inside the building. They'd dumped him in a holding cell a few floors up a staircase and confiscated his backpack. Gavriel assumed the men were guards, though they hadn't charged him with anything and weren't wearing standard uniforms.

During the hours of sitting alone in the cell, Molly consumed his thoughts. Was she scared? Did she try to follow him? He hoped the answer was no to the first question and yes to the second. He would've tried to rescue her had their roles been reversed.

A click of the door unlocking drew Gavriel's attention. The door opened, and in walked his foster dad who frowned and tutted. "You've disappointed me. I didn't think you were such a fool."

"A fool?" Gavriel furrowed his brows. His dad had given him a lot of leeway, more than many foster parents would've. Why the change now? He'd never disapproved of Molly.

His dad produced a paper from his pocket and thrust it at Gavriel. "You know what this says, and you decided you know better. I've raised you to follow the laws, not go against them. Things are going to change. You need more discipline and guidance than I thought."

Gavriel took the paper and glanced at it, his stomach knotting up. It was his Courtship rejection. "I can't be without Molly." His heart ached, as his wrist had when he'd worn the tracker bracelet and gotten too near to her.

"You have to," his dad snapped as he snatched the paper back. "Letting the girl go to wallow and die in the Colony is one thing. I wasn't about to let you go with her. We'll blame this on Henry. Ben is eager to get out of that Courtship, and it'll preserve our reputations."

"I don't care about my reputation. It was my idea not Henry's." Henry had always gone along with Gavriel's plans, starting when they'd met in the Foster Centre. It had been nice having someone reliable and dependable that had his back. Now, Gavriel had lost his girlfriend and best friend on the same night. Molly and Henry barely knew each other and would suffer through their feelings alone.

Gavriel's dad slapped his face. "That's the only time you'll say that."

Gavriel winced and placed his hand over the spot his dad had struck. It stung. He hadn't been hit since he'd been a small child at the Foster Centre. "Why does it matter?"

"Because there's a lot at stake. If you insist on taking the blame, I can have you transferred to the jail and press charges for breaking Courtship and illegal exits laws, but I don't think either of us wants that."

Gavriel lowered his hand and hung his head. Being locked up would keep him away from Molly forever. He had to have a chance of seeing her again. "Fine."

"I knew you'd see reason. Come along."

Gavriel left the tower with his dad, but his life didn't go back to normal. Instead of returning to his routine and school, his dad didn't let him out of the house. Even his lessons were administered in his dad's home office.

Gavriel hadn't intended to thwart the Government. His longing and desperation for Molly had driven him to take a desperate chance for a future with her. He hadn't put much thought into the illegality of it. It wasn't supposed to matter as he hadn't planned on coming back.

After one lesson, a few days later, his dad set a stack of aerial pictures in front of Gavriel. "I have something to show you. This is where they went."

The pictures showed crude wooden huts, with small windows and rudimentary roofs. One picture focused on a specific hut, and Gavriel squinted at it. Why did the drones signal this one out? It didn't look like anything special. Then the reason dawned on him, and he knew whom his dad meant. *Molly and Henry*. "They're staying in the same spot?"

His dad lifted his shoulders in a casual shrug. "As far as we know they're still there. We've had no reports of any vehicles leaving, besides the one that brings food and things in. They haven't tried to come for you, or whatever it is you hoped that girl would do."

Molly. Gavriel winced. He wasn't allowed to say her name, yet he thought about her all the time.

"Do you see that it's best to forget her?"

No. He could never. Molly had to be planning something. He hesitated too long and felt his dad's gaze on him. "I don't—"

His dad grunted. "Go get ready."

Gavriel pushed his chair back with a scrape against the tiles of his dad's office floor. He did it on purpose, not caring that he'd have to buff the marks out later. He went into his room to comb his hair and put on a suit jacket. He wasn't going to be on camera like Ben, and Henry's foster parents, but his dad had told him to be presentable, and he had to put in the effort.

For now, Gavriel would do as he was told and let his anger simmer. His dad had lent his car to some guards to fetch him and tear him from Molly. How could Gavriel forgive him?

He traveled with his dad to a building in Quarter 1 and strode inside. The room they entered was empty except for a white couch that matched the shade of the walls. Gavriel hadn't left his house since going home from the tower. At least this was a change of pace.

Gavriel's dad pushed him towards the couch. "Sit."

Gavriel gritted his teeth to avoid giving a retort as he went and sat on the couch to wait, and his dad left. Piling blame on Henry wasn't on a list of things he wanted to do, but without Molly or Henry, Gavriel had only his dad. He couldn't destroy the one relationship he had left.

After a few moments, in walked Henry's Courtship partner Ben wearing a bored smirk. "At least you're here on time."

"I didn't have a choice," Gavriel muttered. Ben had made it clear he hated Gavriel. Why was he being cordial now?

Ben ignored this remark and shoved a thick stack of papers at Gavriel. "I've heard you're reluctant to blame Henry. Hopefully this will convince you."

Gavriel took the papers and flipped through them. "What are they?"

"Proof of what you did, and the guard report. They found the tracking bracelets. Your ex was careless in throwing hers."

Gavriel cringed at Ben calling Molly his ex. In his mind, they were a temporarily separated couple. She would come back to him. "So what? You're threatening to get me arrested?"

Ben laughed. "It would be the right thing to do. It was *your* fault. You roped Henry into helping you, and the girl was too emotional and desperate to tell you no. However, blaming you doesn't benefit me."

"Threatening me into helping you then. What is it that you want?"

"The same thing your dad wants. Blame Henry. I need an excuse to get out of the Courtship. He's outlasted his usefulness." Every time Ben mentioned Henry, he curled his hands into tight fists and his face flushed with rage.

Gavriel knew there was no love lost on Ben's part when Henry had left. Ben was too selfish for that. However, Henry's departure had affected his ego.

"Seeing as you're both going to do it anyway, I don't know why I have to help."

Ben snorted. "You can go along with our story, or we'll blame both of you. If you ever want to see that girl again, you'll cooperate."

Gavriel narrowed his eyes and pressed his lips together. Ben had no right to dangle Molly in front of him like an elusive reward. He knew they'd be together again, with or without Ben's input.

"You won't if you go to jail. Your dad kept you from it because you can be helpful. It would be easy to send you, and you'd get the real experience this time, not a cozy holding cell in the tower."

"Why do you care? You've never tried to hide that you hate me."

Ben had been the reason Gavriel had seen less of Henry over the past year, and he'd said terrible things to Molly under the guise of helping.

"You were jeopardizing my control of Henry," Ben said. "I almost had him molded to my needs when he decided to leave with you and that girl. I hadn't expected you to be so sentimental over a rejected Courtship."

"I love Molly." She'd been the centre of his world for three years, ever since the day they'd met. That was something Ben would never understand. The centre of Ben's world was himself and his ambition. "I had to try to be with her."

"Love," Ben said with a face that looked like he'd eaten something rotten. "I didn't think anyone was so foolish as to believe in that."

"We're not all like you, Ben. The love I have for her is the most important thing to me."

Ben scoffed. "And you believe she loves you back?"

Gavriel clenched his hands into fists. He'd seen her smile at him and heard what she'd told him. He couldn't have imagined her feelings. She wouldn't have agreed to a Courtship with him if she hadn't loved him. "Of course she does."

Ben flashed a sinister smile. "I wouldn't be so sure."

"You don't know what you're talking about," Gavriel spat. "Trying to make me doubt her isn't going to work."

Ben reached into his pocket and pulled out a stack of photographs, which he thrust at Gavriel. "Take a look and see how confident you are."

Gavriel took the stack. The glee on Ben's face indicated he thought he had something good that would change Gavriel's mind. Gavriel had no intentions on agreeing with Ben about anything.

He flipped the stack over, and the image on top made his heart drop and his body turn cold. The photograph was taken at sunrise and showed Molly and Henry holding hands and smiling at each other. The early morning sun had cast Henry in gold, heightening the tone of his skin and hair and made Molly's eyes sparkle. It made Gavriel want to rip the photographs.

The rest of the stack showed Molly and Henry together, their faces angled at each other, and their hands clasped as they walked. They were always at sunrise, and there was a sheen of sweat on their faces. It was likely from the heat that far south, but Gavriel hated the idea that Molly was doing some daily activity with his supposed best friend and smiling about it. "Where did you get these?"

Ben snatched the pictures from Gavriel. "From my contact in the Colony. He said Henry's turned into Molly's sidekick. Seems she wrapped him around her finger."

Gavriel didn't want to believe Molly had betrayed him intentionally. "You're sure it isn't the other way around? Henry must've thought she needed saving from her heartbreak." She had to be heartbroken being separated from him. He couldn't fault her too much for needing comfort, but he could fault

Henry for taking advantage of her and Molly for clinging to his best friend.

Ben scoffed again. "Henry's too cowardly to have seduced her."

"I won't blame her." He couldn't.

"No one wants you to. She's a child throwing a tantrum. A nobody. We're blaming Henry. The public don't know his nature. It'll be simple enough to paint this as his premeditated plan."

Listening to Ben lay it out made Gavriel almost believe Henry had planned to run away with Molly, getting himself and her away from their intendeds, and had brought Gavriel along as a cover. And now Henry was living with Molly and touching her freely. She belonged at Gavriel's side and had no business looking happy with his best friend who must've charmed her and taken advantage of her emotional state. No matter what Ben said, Gavriel refused to entertain the notion that she'd seduced him. "Fine. I'll go along with it."

"I knew you'd see reason," Ben said, with the first genuine smile Gavriel had ever seen him wear. "For that, I'll give you something else, just to make sure you don't change your mind." He reached into his other pocket and pulled out another, this time smaller, stack of photographs.

This stack was worse than the first for Gavriel. The photographs were of Molly and Henry inside their hut. The first few were of them in the main room, sitting beside each other on the worn-out couch or standing close to each other. The rest were of Molly and Henry in a bedroom. They'd dismantled a set of bunkbeds to place both bunks side by side to form a single, larger bed. The pictures removed all doubt of where they were staying and erased Gavriel's shreds of hope that they weren't as attached as his dad and Ben believed.

Gavriel's vision tinted red. He'd never dreamed that Henry would or could backstab him this way. Molly was his, had always been his. Henry should've stayed with Ben where he belonged. Obviously, years of friendship meant nothing to Henry, and three years of promises meant little to Molly. "I won't change my mind."

Leaving the City had been Gavriel's idea, but blaming Henry would make him feel better. He wanted Henry to hurt, the way he hurt looking at those pictures.

"No," Ben said with a wicked gleam in his eye. "You won't."

Ben left with both sets of pictures, and Gavriel's dad returned a few minutes later. Gavriel expected to go home to more lessons and house arrest, but his dad drove to the tower. This time, Gavriel walked inside on his own feet. He hadn't gotten a look at much of it the first time, or while leaving it, and this time he drank it in. The place was massive. He couldn't see the top of it from the ground.

"We'll be staying here for the next while," Gavriel's dad said. "Word from our source in the Colony is your former friends are helping a group with rebellious tendencies. I need you under close watch, so you don't make any more bad choices."

Gavriel didn't understand what a bunch of Colonists had to rebel over. They'd gotten their way that far south where they could do as they pleased. Before his rejected Courtship, he'd never understood why anyone would want to leave the City at all. "You don't need to worry. I'm not about to join a group of troublemaking criminals."

"I want to believe you, but I already had to haul you back here once."

"I didn't leave to join any rebellions. Those are winless exercises. I just wanted to be with her." The Government was in charge and would continue to be. The fact that Molly and Henry had gotten involved in a traitorous movement against the Government made his blood pressure rise. How had they changed so drastically in such a short time? Maybe they'd always been that way and he'd been blind to it. That was almost worse. Perhaps he was a fool.

"You knew that was illegal. It'll take some time for you to prove you're on the Government's side."

"I get it." Gavriel's longing for Molly had clouded his judgement. It still drove him. He needed her, almost as much as he needed air to breathe and food to live. When he saw her again, he'd forgive her for everything as soon as she denounced the movement she'd been swept up into. Molly had always been impulsive, but she'd see what a mistake she'd made, and then things between her and Gavriel could go back to how they'd been.

"Good."

Inside the tower, his dad led him across the main room and through a door. They climbed the set of stairs to a floor set up like the apartments in Molly's old building. The staircase went up, leading to cells like the one Gavriel had been in. Odd, he thought, to mix comfortable rooms with cells. The metal sheeting was everywhere. This tower was definitely a fortified place.

It was a couple days before Gavriel's dad told him the truth about where they were. The City's Leader lived on the top floor of this tower, and their trusted advisors that made up the Inner Circle, of which Gavriel's dad was one, had offices on the other half of the tower. Gavriel had known his dad had worked for the Government, though he'd been ignorant as to how high up he was. It explained why his dad had pushed so hard to blame Henry. Having a criminal or rebel for a son would impact his position.

"You could've told me all this before," Gavriel said.

"If you hadn't gotten involved with a Rebel's daughter, I might have. Thankfully Ben and his father had a solution for that problem."

In divulging the truth, Gavriel's dad had told him Ben was the reviewer's son, and the whole picture came together in Gavriel's mind. "Why bother putting us under review? Why not just a rejection?"

His dad snorted. "Ben wanted to drag it out to hurt Henry through you. He was always trying to sever you two, no matter how much Bob and I told him Foster Centre kids tend to stick together."

Gavriel didn't like to think of the Foster Centre. He'd been glad to leave it. It had been a dull, boring place with stern guardians and strict routine. Going home with a wealthy Government employee had improved his lot in life immensely, and he'd gotten almost everything he'd wanted. A future with Molly was the first thing denied to him. "I thought he needed me. I was wrong. He just wanted what I had."

His dad rested a hand on Gavriel's shoulder. "You're better off without either of them. That nonsense is behind you. To gain a future worth having, you must be loyal to the Government."

Wanting Molly wasn't nonsense to Gavriel. It never would be, though it had been foolish to keep ties with Henry who had roped Molly into a cause destined to fail. She never would've joined on her own. She needed Gavriel and was acting out in his absence. "I know."

"I think it's time. Make yourself presentable."

Gavriel scrunched his eyebrows together. He'd done nothing except stay in his room for days, and his dad had made no mention of plans. "Time for what?"

"I'll explain on the way once you're ready."

There was no point in arguing. Gavriel went into the bathroom to tame his hair in the mirror. He put on a clean, unwrinkled shirt and joined his dad who nodded in approval and set off down the hall, leaving Gavriel to trail him to the staircase and down.

"The Colonists are becoming trouble. The rest of the Inner Circle wants your input. Our arrest warrant on Henry was a symbolic gesture not likely to gain us anything. He's too cowardly to risk capture."

"Or too cunning." Gavriel didn't see Henry as cowardly, rather as backstabbing and sneaky. "He had me fooled for years."

"That he did," Gavriel's dad said, shooting Gavriel a look. "This meeting isn't about Henry, so put him behind you. It's about her."

"Alright." Gavriel would tell whomever they were meeting whatever they needed. Maybe it would bring Molly back to him.

On the ground floor of the tower, his dad called the elevator, and they rode to a higher floor in the tower on the opposite side from the living quarters. They walked to a spacious room set up like a courtroom for rich people who got arrested and could afford a trial. No one sat at the judge's seat. Three women sat at one bench on the left side of the room, while two men sat across, with an empty seat at the end. One of the men was the Courtship Reviewer, Bob Henson, who'd denied Gavriel and Molly. The man beside him had the same colouring as Henry, a fact Gavriel's brain couldn't process while Bob Henson was glaring at him.

Around the edge of the room was a line of uniformed guards. Gavriel frowned. Did these people see him as so big a threat they needed protection? Or were guards always here?

One of the women, the one on the end with dark skin and eyes, tilted her lips into a cold smile as Gavriel's dad steered him to a table sitting perpendicular to the two benches.

"Carl, you've finally brought your son."

"As he promised days ago," the ash-blonde woman sitting in the middle said. "We've been more than patient."

Gavriel's dad pushed Gavriel onto a seat and gave him a firm look before walking off to join the other men. "He wasn't ready before."

"You're confident he's ready to be helpful now?" the third woman, a few years older than the other two and bearing a strong resemblance to Ben, asked. "It's imperative that we can trust him."

Bob Henson tipped his lips into what might've been a smile had it had any warmth. "Gavriel Kingsley, we've heard some news about your former intended. You knew her better than anyone, save her deceased mother, so we'd like your opinion."

Molly. Gavriel tried not to flinch. Hearing others discuss her was like being pricked by hundreds of needles. "What news?"

Bob Henson turned to Gavriel's dad. "You didn't brief him?"

"Likely wise," the blonde man said. "It didn't leave him time to think up a story."

Bob Henson grunted and focused his attention back on Gavriel. "Word is Miss Birch has become the leader of the Colonist branch of the Rebel Cause and is on route through our City with Henry Connor and a couple runaways they met in the Colony. What do you make of that?"

Gavriel felt his body go cold. Someone had to have put Molly up to this. She wasn't ambitious or a leader of anything, just a temperamental girl acting out because of heartbreak. "She'd never choose to lead such a trivial and unnecessary movement."

Gavriel hated the Colonists who called themselves part of the Rebel Cause. It was one thing for them to take Molly in, but to turn her against the

Government felt like them turning her against him. His dad was part of the Government, and Gavriel couldn't escape it.

Bob Henson shrugged. "Your infatuation might have blinded you to her impulsive and childish tendencies. This is a tantrum of a heartbroken girl who can't deal with her emotions. However, when she arrives, and she will, you must prove whose side you're on. Choose incorrectly, and the consequences will be dire."

There was no doubt to Gavriel about which side he was on. He would never support a movement that opposed everything his father had taught him and that had turned Molly against him. Gavriel wasn't a traitor. "I understand. I'll defend the Government."

The people in the room, who his father later told him were the other members of the Inner Circle making up the Government, debated Gavriel for a while longer. After what felt like hours, they seemed to reach a conclusion, and his dad ushered him from the room.

Instead of returning to their quarters, Gavriel's dad inserted a key in the elevator and pressed the button for the top floor. The elevator lurched upward and Gavriel backed himself into a corner to keep his balance.

"You weren't as much of an embarrassment or disappointment as I feared," his dad said. "I think you might be able to handle the task we're assigning you."

Gavriel didn't bother asking what the task was. He'd find out soon enough. "I am."

When the elevator reached the top floor, it opened into what looked like an office. Before Gavriel could get a thorough view of it, his dad pushed him through the doors, jabbed the door close button and left Gavriel alone. There was a floor to ceiling glass window across from him, which captured his attention while he tried to shove away his fear and slow his pounding heart. Where was he?

"Carl Wessin's orphan foster son," a robotic voice intoned from Gavriel's right.

He swiveled his head to see a figure cloaked from head to toe in black, shapeless robes. There were black gloves on their hands with pointed tips on the fingers, and a black mask under a hood covering their face and hair. The mask had a voice modifier built it, leaving no way to determine the figure's identity.

"I wondered when Carl would take you out of hiding."

Other than the tips of their gloves, they didn't seem to be armed, and a glance around the space showed only the elevator behind Gavriel and a sturdy, likely thick, set of metal doors with no handles or buttons to his left were the exits.

The figure stood unmoving, their mask facing Gavriel. He had no fighting skills, and the self-preservation part of his brain screamed to make himself less of a threat. Besides, there was an obvious answer to whom this was: the City's Leader. Gavriel got on a knee and lowered his head. That was what people used to do to royalty, so it was appropriate here, right? "I suppose he finally trusts me enough."

"Trust," the Leader said in their robotic voice that made it impossible to tell their tone. "That is one question. Another is what to do with you. We cannot leave you idle when the threat comes, but Carl hasn't prepared you for a role of import."

"I'll do whatever needs doing." If this was the Leader, as Gavriel's suspicions indicated, it was best to get on their good side.

The Leader flicked a gloved hand at Gavriel, indicating he should get up, so he did. When he was on his feet, the Leader stepped directly in front of him. "To prove your loyalty, and that you are finished with reckless antics, you will confront the girl, and then summon the guards on whomever from the traitors comes to my chamber. The second part should be simple. The girl is a figure head; they would be rash to send her."

The Leader reached beside Gavriel to insert a key into the elevator panel and pressed the call button. When the doors opened, Gavriel stepped in. This was his cue to leave; anyone could take that hint.

He didn't need a key to select the lowest floor, where he could get off and walk to his room. The traitorous rebels had made a mess for him, and he couldn't wait to see them fail. If it happened in front of Molly, that would be a bonus. She'd come back to him then and realize how manipulated and led astray she'd been.

His reunion with Molly was what fueled Gavriel over the next few days. As his dad updated him on her position, Gavriel tapped into his anger towards the traitors. He couldn't let anyone know his eagerness to see Molly again. It was such a silly movement. Even the guards sending messages of contacts with, or sightings of, Molly and her group found it humorous that the so-called Rebel Cause's best plan was to send her on foot through the City unprotected.

Gavriel would've been worried about her the entire time, had his dad not ordered the Guards to let them come. A better example could be made, he said, if the Government quashed the rebellion personally. Gavriel did worry when the guards lost track of her. She was somewhere in the rich Quarters, having not reached the coast, so close to him and still so far away when he was stuck in the tower, and she was hiding in some dark and cold alley. No rich person was going to shelter a group of runaway teenagers with ties to the

Rebel Cause. Henry's arrest warrant would prevent that if nothing else did.

The Inner Circle and the guards summoned to the tower were on high alert as they waited for Molly and her group. Gavriel spent the time trying to rein in his anger. It didn't work well. Henry was with Molly, which was a stab to Gavriel's heart. Perhaps he'd brought it on himself by enlisting Henry's help getting out of the City. That made it worse, and he'd never dreamed his best friend would come with them.

Finally, word came that Molly and her companions were approaching the coast. Gavriel had long been ready for this moment and walked with his dad to wait with Bob Henson behind the large entry room's door. Ben had insisted on greeting the group first and alone.

There'd been nothing Gavriel could do to change it, with Henry being Ben's ex, so he bided his time waiting for the signal. It felt like hours until Bob Henson got his son's summons and went into the entry. Gavriel and his dad would come last of their group, before the Leader. The rest of the Inner Circle had opted to stay out of it, seeing Molly as too little of a threat to warrant taking personal action. If it hadn't been for Ben's insistence on taunting Henry face-to-face, guards would've arrested Molly and her group at the Gate and Gavriel wouldn't have had this chance to see her.

"Wipe that hope from your mind," Gavriel's dad said. "She's a troublemaker with no place in your life."

"I know." Gavriel tried to better conceal his anticipation of reuniting with Molly, but he'd always struggled with hiding his emotions. "I just need to see her for closure." It was partly true, though he had other ideas about how their reunion should go.

"You need to do what the Leader told you, nothing more."

His dad received the signal, opened the door, and walked through first.

Gavriel followed. They stopped beside Bob and Ben, and Gavriel scanned the group in front of them. There was an older blonde girl and black-haired boy, whom Gavriel didn't know. They were unimportant, and his eyes slid over them to find Henry and Molly standing together.

Gavriel's heartbeat sped up. Molly was as beautiful as the last time he'd seen her, though she had circles under her eyes and tension in her shoulders. Gavriel used his self restraint to keep from going to her and taking her into his arms. His father's insult, directed to Molly more than him, didn't register in his ears. His eyes stayed on Molly, and he saw her lips move, though he couldn't hear her words. She wasn't looking at him, and she grabbed Henry's hand and clung to it, before something sparked in her eyes, and she yanked her hand away.

Gavriel gritted his teeth, and his nostrils flared. "You shouldn't have come back, Molly." He didn't want her here touching Henry. His heart couldn't bear it and broke into millions of pieces from the sight in front of him and the look in Henry's eyes as he kept glancing at Molly. Gavriel wanted her, more than he'd ever wanted anything. He had held out miniscule bits of hope that Ben's reports were exaggerated, or that they'd helped each other through grief. He'd imagined Molly running to him with apologies for not coming back to him sooner. That fantasy vanished, and with it his friendship with Henry.

She kept her eyes away, looking at anything except Gavriel, and made no move to leave Henry's side. "I had to."

"No. You should have stayed away. It's obvious I didn't mean anything to you. It would have hurt less if I never saw you again."

Learning to Be Family

Henry

In the weeks since Henry shot Carl Wessin, he hadn't left Jack's house. Leaving meant dealing with the attention of strangers calling him The Vanquisher. Titles and recognition suited Molly, not him. She came alive when there was a crowd to rally or a cause to champion. Henry would just let someone down.

After a couple months, Jack came to the room Henry shared with Molly. She was out getting their rations for the week, and Henry had expected to be alone. He looked up at Jack in acknowledgement of his presence. One thing he'd learned from the Newsomes was not to ignore an adult.

Jack stayed in the doorway and gave Henry a small, closed-lipped smile. "Your dad's here to see you."

Henry wrinkled his eyebrows. He hadn't seen Malcolm since the tower nor heard from him. He hadn't expected to. "Why?"

Jack lifted his shoulders in a shrug. He and Molly shared much of their colouring and features, yet they were so different in temperament. "He said he wants to speak to you."

Henry held back a sigh and followed Jack upstairs. If his dad had come, there was a reason. By the window in the main room, standing in the mid-morning light, was Malcolm, who turned to gaze at Henry.

Jack grabbed his keys. "I'll go pick up Molly and give you two some privacy." He put his shoes on and practically fled the house.

Henry hadn't shared his sister's animosity towards their dad, but he never knew how to act around him. Reginald Newsome hadn't helped him practice that.

"You look tired," his dad said. "Have you slept alright?"

"Yeah, I have." It was a half true. He slept fine when he didn't have nightmares. They plagued him multiple times a week, featuring the Newsomes, the Foster Centre, Ben and the events in the tower.

His dad walked over to the couch, sat and patted the cushion beside him. "It's just from hiding out here then. What are you worried about?"

Henry should've known that Jack would tell Malcolm. They'd been friends since they were Molly's age. He sat next to his dad and let his shoulders slouch. "Molly handles attention better than I do. If I go out there, people are going to realize I'm not a hero."

Malcom rested his hand on Henry's shoulder. "You don't need to put so much pressure on yourself. You're only one person. Besides, the public's focus is shifting to what happens next. Jack's agreed to lead, temporarily."

Molly had pressured Jack about that since she and Henry moved in. She'd be pleased to know that he finally gave in.

"Is he kicking me and Molly out and sent you to tell us?"

Malcolm shook his head and lowered his hand. "No. I came on my own to ask you a couple things."

"Okay. Ask away."

"How'd you feel about being a guard again? I'm overhauling the Guard Corps to make it less hostile and more inclusive. There's a spot for you if you want it."

Henry could see appeal in the idea. He had the training and skills, and Malcolm was in charge, but that life hadn't appealed to him the first time around and still didn't. "I don't. I'm sorry."

Malcolm dipped his head. "I expected as much. The real reason I came was because Valerie has agreed to move in with me. Will you help her get settled?"

Valerie had agreed to leave the Colony to live with Malcolm? Henry had never thought that would happen. The rumours about people migrating back to the City from the Colony and supply runs dwindling must've been true. "Okay."

Henry wanted to see his sister. That's how he ended up packing a bag with things he needed for an overnight trip when Molly walked into their room.

She stopped short and raised her eyebrows. "Where are you going?"

Henry stuffed the last item into the bag and tugged the zipper closed. She hadn't asked if he was leaving her. She trusted him to know he could never do that. "To help Valerie settle in. She's moving in with my dad."

Molly sat on the bed and laughed. "Likely to be closer to Max. You're sure your dad's not trying to convince you to do the same?"

He sat beside her and lifted her hand. "I'd never do that without you."

Molly sucked in a deep breath and squeezed Henry's hand. "My dad told me he's going to be temporary Leader, and one of his first acts will be to revamp the Courtship process. Only people already married, or closely related to their intended will be denied."

Standing across from Molly and reciting his vows had been the best and most nerve-wracking day of Henry's life. It hadn't been legal nor meant anything to the people not in attendance. Molly wore his mother's jewelry and a ring from her grandmother, but those were just jewels, silver and gold. They had no meaning in the absence of a legal Courtship. Living with her now was technically a law violation, and Jack was gifting them a way to fix it. "At least our application will get approved. I know Clinic Day is months away, but—"

"That's the best part," Molly said with a beaming smile. "He's going to legally recognize marriages performed in the Colony under the former Courtship laws. We don't have to apply. We'll get our paperwork in the mail once there's a new Courtship Reviewer."

"We could still have a big wedding." Molly thrived under the spotlight. His proposal had been intimate, and their wedding rushed. He wanted to make it up to her. "Take our time planning it and have everyone there. Like Gavriel. You could even buy a fancy dress."

Molly adjusted her position on the bed, rested her forehead on his and crossed her wrists behind his neck. "I don't need a fancy wedding. I have you, and that's all I want. Don't you think it was perfect the first time?"

Even with his nerves, it had been perfect. He wouldn't go back and change anything. "Yes."

Molly kissed him, making his lips tingle. "The only weddings in our future are likely to be our friends'."

Henry smirked. None of them were near to having weddings.

"What time are you leaving tomorrow?" she asked.

"Early. It'll take all day to move Valerie in." Henry hadn't seen the house since the night he'd slept on the floor with Valerie, Jax and Molly. A layer of dust and crime had coated the entire place then. He wondered what condition it was in now.

In the morning, after eating a quick breakfast and giving Molly a kiss goodbye, Henry hefted his bag and followed Malcolm outside. Parked on the wide Outskirts' street was a shining black car. The solar panels built into its roof gleamed in the sunlight. Henry was still growing accustomed to the relative wealth his dad had.

He tucked his bag in the trunk and claimed the passenger seat for the quick drive into the City.

"What do you plan to do if not the Guard Corps?" Malcolm asked as he steered to the road going up the side of the Apartment Districts.

Henry hadn't decided, but an idea keeping lingering in his brain, having taken root from what Molly said to him once. "I'd like to work in the archives."

"Your mom was the academic type. She'd be proud of you."

"What else was she like?" All he knew about her was a few pieces from what Valerie told him, and her name. He kept her picture on the nightstand in his and Molly's bedroom. Jack had gotten him a frame for it, and it sat next to one of Molly's mom. It was fitting, considering they'd been best friends.

"A lot like you. She was braver than she credited herself with and always trying to help other people."

Henry couldn't miss the woman he didn't remember, though she'd left a hole in his life he was trying to fill. "I wish I'd known her."

Malcolm exhaled deep. "I do too."

Henry repositioned his gaze onto the windshield. Valerie remembered Henry as a little kid and their dad, which left Henry feeling inferior at times, but she shared a mutual hole their mom left and no memory of her.

Malcolm turned down the street leading to Max's apartment. When he parked, and they went inside, he knocked on Max's door.

Max opened the door and ran a hand over his rumpled curls to smooth them. "You're just in time. Val's been here overnight and has reorganized all my stuff."

"Max!" Valerie yelled from deeper in the apartment. "Who's at the door?"

Max sighed and turned his head to reply. "Your family."

Henry heard a thump and his sister's running footsteps. She barreled through Max's apartment and almost collided with Max when she tried to stop herself at the door.

"You got Henry to come?" Valerie asked with a raised eyebrow.

Henry's face fell. Had Valerie expected and wanted to be alone with Malcolm? He supposed he could take a bus back to the Gate and walk to Jack's house.

Malcolm nodded.

Henry hated himself for not seeing what this was. Malcolm was using him as a buffer between himself and Valerie.

Valerie beamed, grabbed Henry's wrist and yanked him into Max's apartment. "Thanks."

Henry tugged himself free from his sister's grasp.

Max smirked, seeming to enjoy the scene unfolding around him. He wouldn't rescue Henry.

"You're welcome," Malcolm said.

"I'm happy you're here, Henry," Valerie said. "Now Max has help to move my stuff."

Henry furrowed his brows. "You're not going to carry any of it?" First his dad was using him, now his sister. He should've stayed at Jack's.

Valerie laughed. "No. I'm going to help Dad pack it in the car. Max'll show you where my stuff is."

Henry sighed as his sister skipped into the hall.

Max set off towards his bedroom with a wave over his shoulder for Henry to follow. "Not eager to help your sister?"

"I'd do anything for Val. I'm just not sure she or our dad wants my help more than a safety net between them."

Max chuckled, making Henry frown. He hadn't tried to joke.

"You didn't even know they existed a few months ago. Finding each other doesn't make you an instantly perfect family."

Ever since Henry had been at the Foster Centre, he'd wanted a family. When the Newsomes took him home, he'd believed for a moment he'd gotten one. Then they'd laid out their rules and spent years belittling and criticizing him. They hadn't loved him, and neither had Ben. Henry hadn't had a family until he married Molly. "I don't think we know how to be one."

"You can ponder it while you help me move this stuff."

Max was in his bedroom standing over boxes that had to be Valerie's. Henry hadn't realized his sister owned so much stuff, but she had spent seven years in the Colony and obviously accumulated possessions she didn't want to part with.

Henry stooped and grabbed the nearest box. It was heavy, and he grunted when he straightened up. "What's in them?" he asked as he followed Max, carrying another box without complaint, through the apartment.

"Whatever she claimed in her Colony house. She'd packed them before I got there."

Henry would have words with his sister on how to pack without overloading boxes. She must've gone to the Market for them. Suitcases and bags were in short supply in the Colony, especially with so many people returning to the City.

Henry was grateful for the elevator in Max's building, and that Max lived on a high enough floor to use it. It took four trips for him and Max to transfer all of Valerie's stuff down to Malcolm's car. It would've been easier if Malcolm had gone to get her from the Colony instead of Max, or if Max had taken her directly to Malcolm's house. "Why did Val come to your apartment instead of straight to dad's house?"

Max jabbed the elevator call button for the last trip down. "She wanted to stay here."

This was a detail no one had told Henry. "Dad said she agreed to move in with him."

Max huffed. "It's either that or find her own place, and Val has no money. You know she can't stay with me."

Henry felt for his sister. She'd called Max to take her from a dying Colony, and the only place she could go was Malcolm's. Val and Max weren't even dating, which made living together illegal, and Clinic Day was many months away. "You didn't tell her on the way?"

Max shrugged. "I didn't have to. Malcolm sent me to get her. That doesn't mean she didn't want some private time here. You must understand that."

Henry did understand. If he'd been in Valerie's position, he would've wanted some private time with Molly, no matter the risk.

The elevator came, and Henry and Max rode down with the last of Valerie's things. Outside, Max handed the box in his arms to Malcolm and hugged Valerie. "Good luck."

Valerie grinned up at Max when he released her. "Thanks for everything. See you soon?"

He dipped his head and walked backward, towards his apartment building. "When you're settled."

Henry added the last of Valerie's boxes into the trunk. His sister claimed the passenger seat, so he got in the back, next to a stack of the smaller boxes and affixed his eyes on the view. The last time he'd been at Malcolm's house it had been dark out and he'd worn his guard uniform. There hadn't been an opportunity to get a good view of it or the neighbourhood.

Seeing it in daylight revealed how much money his dad had. The neighbouring yards were lush and immaculate, and there was no dust or grime anywhere. The Newsomes would've salivated at the chance to charm their way into Henry's life now and take advantage of Malcolm's money.

The outside of the house was clean of dust, and the windows shined like someone had washed them, but the yard still had patchy grass with no flowers, shrubs or bushes.

Henry heard his sister gasp. She unbuckled her seatbelt and fled the car as soon as Malcolm parked. With a groan, Henry pressed the release on his seatbelt and went after her.

Valerie stood in the middle of the lawn, her head tilted back so she could gaze at the house. "It looks almost like I remember."

"I've been working on restoring it," Malcolm said from behind them. "I always wanted to claim it again."

"Why let it go to ruin in the first place?" Henry asked.

Malcolm hung his head and inhaled a deep breath. "Part of the deal Scarlet offered me was that I had to give up everything that had a connection to Amelia. I couldn't part with the house completely, so I filed it under my parents' names and left it untouched. Scarlet loved knowing it was in ruin."

Henry had never heard Malcolm mention his parents. He'd assumed they were dead, and by the look on his sister's face, she'd thought the same. "Are they still alive?"

Malcolm heaved a sigh and let his shoulders sag. "No. They never knew I filed the house in their names."

"Did you tell them you were leaving us?" Valerie asked.

There was an edge to her voice Henry hadn't heard in months.

"No," Malcolm said. "I couldn't."

Valerie shot Henry a glance from the corner of her eye and marched to the door. "Let's go inside. Come on Henry."

Henry jogged across the lawn and followed Valerie inside. It was less awkward than more questions about grandparents he couldn't remember. He stopped dead in his tracks when he crossed the threshold. The last time he'd been in the house, it had been devoid of furniture and caked in dust and dirt. The grime was gone; there was fresh paint on the walls and some pieces of furniture filled the rooms Henry could see. Malcolm had put a lot of work into the place or hired someone else to.

"There's still a lot to do," Malcolm said from behind Henry.

Valerie had disappeared from the front entrance, and Henry could hear her footsteps on the stairs. He swallowed and looked at Malcolm. There was nothing Henry wanted more, now that he'd married Molly, than to feel like a family with his dad and sister. The problem was making it happen.

"Come get Valerie's bags with me, and you can say whatever's on your mind."

Henry wasn't sure how, but Malcolm had guessed his thoughts. "Okay."

It was on the second trip between the car and the house that Henry collected himself enough to form coherent words. "I don't know how to do this."

Being looked at with eyes the same green as his own unsettled Henry. When the Newsomes had scolded him and sneered at him, he'd never seen himself in their expressions. Malcolm was gazing at Henry with wrinkled brows, and no scowls or frowns in sight. Henry knew how to deal with anger and disappointment directed his way from parental figures, not this.

"You're going to need to be clearer. How to do what, Henry?"

Henry pushed the house's door open and added the box in his arms to the stack on the floor. He hung his head. If Molly was here, she would've given him courage. It was difficult to muster on his own. "I want us to be a family, but I don't know how."

Malcolm placed the box in his arms with the others. "There's no instruction book or rules to follow on that. We can only figure it out as we go."

That made it easier for Henry to fail, and he failed often. "What if that isn't good enough? I've been a disappointment enough times in my life." He'd been a constant one to the Newsomes.

Malcolm regarded him with a tilt to his head that made Henry feel like he was being studied. "Have you disappointed yourself?"

Henry wobbled on his feet. There'd been so little he'd done for himself, and his expectations of himself were nonexistent. Growing up, what he'd wanted hadn't mattered. Looking back on it, he wished he could've been braver and more self-assured. No one had given him the tools. "A bit."

Malcolm beckoned Henry over. "Come here."

Malcolm didn't use the same forceful tone Reginald Newsome had used, but Henry went anyway, keeping his head down. He knew better than to disregard an order.

Malcolm nudged Henry's chin up with his fingers, forcing Henry to meet his eyes. "You aren't Henry Newsome or Henson. You're *my* son. If you're disappointed in yourself, it's my fault, not yours or the people who raised you, and I'm sorry for causing you pain. What The Newsomes wanted and expected from you doesn't matter."

Henry chewed on his bottom lip as Malcolm lowered his hand. "I wish I'd been braver." *Like Molly and Valerie.*

"You were a child. You're not a coward. I've seen you be brave."

"Why do you do that to yourself?" Valerie asked.

Henry hadn't heard his sister come back downstairs, yet she was at the bottom of the staircase, her eyes on him and her mouth in a frown. The truthful answer to her question was that he'd learned to admit and accept blame and to agree with his foster parents' negative view of him. As a nine-year-old thrust into an abusive environment, that was the only coping mechanism he'd had that had lessoned the punishment and admonishment. "Because it's true."

Valerie crossed the room, grasped Henry's arm and shot their dad a glance. "Can you get the rest of my stuff?"

Malcolm dipped his head. "Of course."

Valerie dropped Henry's arm and picked up a box. "Come upstairs with me."

Henry followed his sister. The stairs creaked, and the tiles in the upstairs hallway were chipping, as was the paint. There was no visible dirt, yet the space still needed a lot of work.

Valerie led him to his childhood bedroom where he could spend the night, then took him to the next bedroom, which had been hers. Malcolm had stripped the walls in both rooms since the last time Henry had seen them, leaving the spaces as blank canvasses. Henry couldn't remember living in his childhood room, so the bareness of it didn't bother him.

If it bothered Valerie, she didn't show it. She put her box down, closed the door and rounded on him. "You're worrying me."

"How?" He hadn't done anything since the tower. What was there to worry about?

"You think I don't know you've been hiding in Jack's house? I asked Dad to bring you here, and you show up looking terrified that we're going to hurt you. Why wouldn't I be worried?"

"You asked him?" Henry had thought it was Malcolm's idea.

Valerie rolled her eyes. "He was going to anyway. We both want to see you, and you can't hide forever. I'm surprised Molly and Jack haven't dragged you out by now."

Henry wasn't angry at Malcolm like Valerie used to be, but the man was a stranger to him. In a way, Jack was a stranger to Molly. She'd known he existed, though their only correspondence for years had been through mail. Despite that, Molly was herself around Jack in a way Henry wanted to be with Malcolm. "I'm sorry."

His sister grumbled. "Don't apologize to appease me. After what we went through, I thought you'd trust me. We aren't going to hurt you."

Henry sighed. "Aren't you scared of messing up? Or letting Dad down?"

Valerie pressed her lips into a line and tossed her head. "No. Dad let us down already, and I let you down. We're like three puzzle pieces that were scattered and beaten up and found their way back together. Don't try to be perfect, Henry. Dad and I aren't. You can blame us for your childhood. It's not your fault."

Henry's eyes watered, and he blinked to chase away the tears. "I don't want to blame you."

She swiped his tears with her thumb. "Then don't. Just promise to go easier on yourself."

"I'll try." Henry meant it. It was long past time to forget what the Newsomes had taught him, however difficult that would be.

When the boxes were all in Valerie's room, she shooed Henry out so she could unpack in relative peace. He went to find Malcolm, who was in the kitchen standing in front of an open cabinet.

"Dad?" Henry asked.

Malcolm turned his head towards Henry. "We need chocolate."

Henry's eyebrows show up. "Chocolate?" Only with Ben, and once in the Colony, had he ever eaten any.

"Yes, for the surprise I want to make your sister. Do you want to come to the store with me?"

"Sure." What else was he going to do? Sit alone while his sister unpacked?

"Great. I'll go tell Valerie we're going."

Henry went outside while Malcolm went upstairs. The rich Quarters were peaceful and quiet compared to living in the Outskirts or the Apartment Districts. People living here had so much space.

Malcolm exited the house, car keys in hand. "You should learn to drive. Then you can come into the City on your own."

Valerie knew how, and Molly had done it once. There was no reason Henry couldn't. If he'd had more years in the Guard Corps, they might've taught him. "I'd like to."

Malcolm and Henry got in the car, and he backed it out of the driveway. "Good. I'll talk to Jack about it once your sister is more settled."

"What's the surprise you're making?" Henry asked.

Malcolm flashed a wistful smile as he steered down the street. "She probably doesn't remember, but as a little girl, she always wanted chocolate pancakes. Your mom and I used to take turns making them, and later, I did it alone."

"Did Mom like to cook?" The Foster Centre had taught Henry how to cook as a useful skill. He hadn't been meant to enjoy it like he did.

"I don't think she did before the ration system. Her parents couldn't afford much."

"Oh." Henry had wanted something in common with his mom. If he could never know her, at least there would've been something of hers to share.

"She found love for it when she had access to better ingredients and some seasoning. It took an entire afternoon to grocery shop when we first got married. I couldn't get her out of the spice section."

Henry felt himself smile while picturing his mother glued to the spice section, sniffing them all and gazing in wonder. Perhaps they had a common interest after all.

...

The store Malcolm drove to was large and immaculate. The customers leaving had carts stocked with more than anyone in the Apartment Districts ever got with their rations. Even Ben hadn't bought this much food.

Malcolm took a basket. "If you see anything you or Molly want, feel free to grab it."

Henry had no intention of doing that, until he and Malcolm were in the confectionary section. On the top shelf of the chocolate aisle there was a jar labelled 'hot chocolate mix'. Henry reached up and grasped one to read it up close. The label advertised it as just needing hot water, which was a change from the recipe Ben had taught him.

"Is that for you or Molly?" Malcolm asked. He had a sack of chocolate pieces in the basket alongside a jar of syrup.

"Both, if it's any good." If not, Henry wouldn't force Molly to drink it, though she would offer.

Malcolm held the basket out for Henry to drop the mix in. "Won't know for sure until you try it. Want anything else?"

"I don't think so."

"Alright."

The checkout experience reminded Henry of shopping with Ben as Malcolm paid in cash since their items weren't on the ration list. Ben had done so often, though he'd taken full advantage of the ration list.

Valerie was still unpacking her things when Henry and Malcolm returned. Malcolm went straight to the kitchen to get out a mixing bowl, spoon and frying pan. He was pulling out ingredients and setting them on the counter when Henry walked in.

Even if Valerie hadn't shooed him out of her room, Henry would've gravitated to the kitchen. He wanted this chance to feel closer to his parents. "I'll help."

Malcolm gave him a bright smile and beckoned him closer. "Great."

Henry walked up to his dad, who thrust ingredients, including real sugar, and measuring spoons across the counter. He scooped out amounts Malcolm instructed, added them to the bowl and mixed. The batter smelled so good it made his mouth water.

Henry was tempted to write the recipe down, but he and Molly couldn't replicate it with their reliance on rationed foods. They had no money coming in, and Jack was funding Molly's expedited correspondence program for her high school degree. The Guard Corps had funded it for Henry, so it was time to do something productive that would help his wife and take pressure off Jack. "Dad?" he asked as Malcolm fried some of the batter. "Do you know anything about applying for jobs?"

Malcolm turned his head and looked Henry in the eye. "It's been a while, but I think I could help."

"Thanks. I just think it's time I help Molly instead of being someone for her to take care of."

"If she's anything like her parents, she won't see you that way."

Molly always had a rosy view of Henry, and he wanted to live up to it. "She still deserves better than living in Jack's Outskirts house though." Maybe if he got a job at the archives they could move into an apartment. Those were small, but it would be their own space, and Jack would have his privacy back.

Henry scooped some of the batter and poured it into the second frying pan. He looked up and caught Malcolm gazing at him. Henry frowned. What had he done wrong?

"Jack would never send either of you away, but you're right. You two need your own place. I'll keep an eye out for houses that go on the market."

Henry blinked, and his jaw dropped. "A house? We can't afford—"

"No, you can't currently, but I can."

"You want to buy us a house?" That was a debt Henry would never be able to repay, nor was it something he wanted dangled over his head for decades.

Malcolm put his hand on Henry's shoulder and gave it a squeeze. "I never wanted you, or Valerie, to suffer and grow up poor. Think of this as using part of your share of our family's wealth."

Henry flipped the pancake. "Alright, but I don't want to tell Molly right away. It would be better as a surprise. Maybe for our anniversary." She had enough to deal with that didn't involve house shopping, and Henry trusted Malcolm enough to find a decent place.

Malcolm got a plate from the cupboard and slid the first cooked pancakes onto it. "That should be doable."

Henry wanted that time to get to a place where he could afford the monthly costs of having a house. "Perfect."

Henry and Malcolm cooked the rest of the pancakes and stacked them on a serving tray. Henry had just set empty plates on the dining table when he heard his sister's footsteps enter the room.

She took a deep sniff of the air. "Something smells good."

"Pancakes. Dad said he used to make them for you."

Valerie gazed at him with soft eyes and a closed-lip smile. "For us, you mean."

Henry shrugged. "I thought you might remember. I don't."

Valerie walked across the dining room and wrapped her arms around Henry. "It's okay. We'll make new family memories. Next time, you can bring your wife." She unwrapped Henry and went into the kitchen.

Bring Molly here? Henry wasn't opposed to the idea. His family was Molly's, by way of their marriage. Why should he keep the two separate?

Henry sat at the table with his dad and sister and dug into some of the pancakes.

Valerie doused hers in syrup. Her eyes rolled back from pleasure as she chewed the first bite. "You didn't have to do this for me. Just letting me stay here is enough."

Malcolm got a bite of pancake on his fork and brought it to his lips. "I thought it might remind you of when you were little."

"I remember quite a bit," Valerie said.

The two years in age between Henry and his sister meant she had memories of the time before their separation. Henry had nothing from his early childhood he could call a memory. It was impossible to relate to his sister as she reminisced with Malcolm, so Henry kept quiet.

Valerie and Malcolm had an easy rapport with each other. They remembered what it was like to be a family, and Henry didn't. He didn't fit in here, no matter how nice Valerie was to him.

"Henry? Henry!?"

He blinked and looked up from his plate to see Valerie staring at him with concern in her eyes. Malcolm had left his seat without Henry noticing.

"Are you okay?"

Henry set down his fork. "I can't relate to Dad the way you can."

"He doesn't expect you to."

"That's the issue. The only parental figures I remember having always had clear, usually unattainable, expectations of me. With Dad, I don't know what to do or what he wants."

Valerie pressed her lips together. "The Newsomes were terrible parents. It's not healthy to spend your life chasing impossible goals in the aim of pleasing unpleasable people."

"That's all I know how to do." It had been the same with Ben, and even Gav had expected Henry to be something he wasn't. Molly was the exception. She never asked impossible things of him.

Valerie frowned. "I'm sorry I didn't try harder to save you. If I had, maybe we could've run away together."

"You don't need to be sorry for that." Henry had never blamed her.

Valerie's eyes misted, and she blinked to clear them. "I felt guilty. It helped thinking that you might've gone to live with a nice couple. When I found out otherwise, I wanted to thrash them."

"I'm trying to forget them." He had to in order to stop the nightmares and Molly's worry. He wanted to focus on his family. Haunting of his past weren't welcome or helpful.

Malcolm returned to the dining room and set a mug in front of each

Valerie and Henry. "As you should."

Henry hadn't realized Malcolm had heard his conversation with Valerie. It didn't matter. He picked up his mug, which was warm and held a steaming, brown liquid. Henry took a sip, and smooth, chocolate flavoured liquid slid down his throat. This was better than the recipe Ben had taught him. "Is this from the mix?"

Malcolm, who'd retaken his seat, shook his head. "An old recipe my mom and Amelia came up with."

Valerie shot Henry a look over her mug as she drank. "Will you tell us more about Mom? I want to know everything."

Henry did too and sat up straighter in his seat.

"After we clean this up, I'll tell you whatever you want to know."

Valerie emptied her mug, grabbed her plate off the table and stood up, giving Henry a glance that he should do the same. "You can dry, little brother."

Henry groaned as he grabbed his plate and followed Valerie into the kitchen. She stood at the sink and had turned the water on. "Do you want me to call you 'big sister'?"

She flicked water from the sponge at him. "Older sibling privileges include choosing nicknames. I'm vetoing that one."

Henry flung his arm up to shield his face. "Whatever you say, Val."

She threw the dish towel at him and plucked his plate from his hand. "That one's okay."

Henry grinned as his sister scrubbed the plates and handed them to him to dry and set on the drying rack. Maybe being siblings was easier than he thought. He liked it best when they joked and teased each other.

After doing the dishes, Valerie and Henry found Malcolm sitting on the couch in the living room, rolling a gold ring in the palm of his hand. It was smaller in diameter than the matching one on his finger. When Henry got closer, he could see tiny diamonds all around the band.

Valerie sat to Malcolm's left, leaving Henry the space on his right. "Is that Mom's?" Valerie asked, leaning in to get a closer look.

"Yes. One of her things I couldn't part with."

Henry hadn't seen Malcolm wear a wedding band before. If put in the same position, Henry wouldn't have parted with his or Molly's either. "Where did you hide them?"

"The same place I hid the pictures and the jewelry I gave you. In a box under the floorboards in Amelia's old office. The neighbours across the street can't see into that room through the windows."

Without knowing, Henry, Valerie, Jax and Molly had slept on the floor over Malcolm's hiding spot. He'd been close to his mom's memory then and been oblivious to it. "Is there more in it?"

"A couple things," Malcolm said. "Documents, mostly."

"Show us?" Valerie asked, her face lit up like a child invited on a grand adventure.

"Alright," Malcolm stood and pocketed Amelia's ring. "Follow me."

...

A metal box with a latch on the lid was under a tile in the back corner of the room. It looked big enough to store a paid of guard boots. Malcolm had cleared the dust from the room, though it remained empty of furniture and had the same flooring and faded paint as the last time Henry had been in it. Malcolm had crouched to retrieve the box, and he stayed in that position to open it. When the lid was open, he reached inside to remove a folder and then stood up. "This is the last of it."

He opened the folder and slid out a stack of documents. Henry joined his sister in standing close to Malcolm to see what he flipped through. The first was something Henry had had with Ben: a Courtship acceptance letter and Courtship papers. Both Malcolm's and Amelia's were in the box. They weren't necessary after a marriage and must have been sentimental to Henry's parents. Next was their marriage license, with signatures still legible.

After the marriage license, there were only two small cards left. Malcolm sighed as he picked them up and held them out for Henry and Valerie to see.

One was Amelia's ID card, and the other was a proof of parentage card documenting Amelia Connor as their mother. It was the first time Henry had seen her name in print, and next to her surname on the proof of parentage care, in brackets, was her maiden name: Ruby.

Henry heard his sister sniff and saw her swipe across her eyes with her wrist. Underneath their mom's name and birthdate were Valerie's and Henry's. The ID card and proof of parentage card were useless after Amelia's death in the eyes of the Government, good only for proving to Valerie and Henry whom their mom had been.

"You loved Mom a lot, didn't you?" Valerie asked. "Why else would you keep all this?"

Malcolm blinked, sending tears leaking down his cheeks. "I did, but your mom was important to other people. Scarlet Everbee hated her for more than marrying me. Preserving Amelia's memory the best I could was my way of carrying on her legacy."

"Important to whom?" Henry asked. He'd thought Malcolm had saved all this as proof for his children and out of sentimentality. Yet, Scarlet Everbee had said Amelia had Rebel Cause sympathies. How did these documents tie into that? "Was she a Rebel Cause member?"

Malcolm set his eyes on Henry, and they emitted warmth. It was nothing like the judgement Reginald Newsome had shown Henry. "She named it. Jack can tell you the story as well as I can, if not better. As could Max's parents," he said with a glance at Valerie.

"What?" Valerie asked with a blink.

Malcolm inhaled a deep breath. "Before the Rebel Cause existed, there were fractured movements trying to make change, some more effective than others, though none very successful. Jack got Amelia involved, and she saw how to unite the different segments and solve the biggest issue at the time. She was a lot like you both of you: a fighter for those she cared about. She could've been a leader in the Rebel Cause, but she chose a role in the background."

"You kept all this as and joined the Rebel Cause as revenge against Scarlet Everbee?" Valerie asked.

Malcolm shook his head. "I helped your mom and our friends establish the ration system. It replaced the Food Laws, which they likely tell kids in school these days how awful they were, and the Government would take credit for changing the system, of course. Saving the documents was for you two, and for the Rebel Cause record."

Henry hadn't known the parallels between his life and his dad's or that he'd learned part of their story in history class. He'd done what Malcolm had, in helping Molly lead the Rebel Cause. No one had told him his own mother had formed it, but that fact brought it full circle. And, if forced to forget Molly, Henry would hide things of hers too. Malcolm had honoured his and Amelia's love for each other, and for their children. It was the best thing a parental figure had ever done for Henry. He squared his shoulders, inhaled a deep breath and hugged Malcolm. "Thank you for showing us."

The First Date

Max

Max clutched the handhold hanging from the ceiling of the crowded bus. Maybe others would find it odd, but he liked riding the bus. Perhaps because he couldn't when he was on duty as a Guard or engaged in activities for the Rebel Cause. This one was on the few times he ventured out of his apartment for something personal that wasn't an errand or a meeting with Sage.

The bus emptied as it headed north into the rich Quarters. Most people going that direction were too young to drive, and there were others that went that way for work. Max had a different reason.

He hadn't expected his life to change as much and as fast as it had when Jack Birch asked him to keep an eye on his daughter. The changes hadn't come only from watching and helping Molly overturn the old Government. No, an emotionally wounded blonde girl had worked her way into his life.

Max had heard stories of Valerie before meeting her. She'd been the snappy, guarded, troublemaker fighting for influence in the Colony. Then, when he'd given her Malcolm's letter, he'd caught a glimpse of the sad, broken and vulnerable version of herself she'd tried to conceal.

There were passion and love in Valerie too. He'd seen it in that Colony house. Being around Henry and having a purpose had brought it out of her. Max's purpose there had been to watch and protect Molly.

Protecting people had been a commonality that brought Max and Valerie together. He'd thought after their kiss outside the tower that he'd never see her again, and he'd devoted his energy to helping Malcolm reform the Guard Corps, letting work consume him. That was until the day he'd fetched Valerie from the Colony. She'd spent one night at Max's apartment then, and he hadn't wanted to let her leave.

Even the one night was risky. There were still laws against people not in a Courtship or married living together. Still, it had taken him days to put his things back where they belonged after her reorganization. He didn't want to lose her fingerprints on his life.

Valerie was living with Malcolm now, which was where Max was headed. When the bus reached his stop, he gathered his courage as he walked the short distance to their house. Perhaps she'd never felt more than a passing affection for him or had sought comfort from him after the horrible situation with Kayden. The only form of love Valerie had known for most of her life was the unhealthy possessive obsession Kayden had shown towards her.

Henry and Malcolm were doing their best to change that, but they were family. Max wanted to show her what romantic love could be, and he wanted to do it while he still had the chance and time before Clinic Day.

He knocked once on the Connors' front door and waited, hoping Valerie would answer the door and not Malcolm. It turned out to be neither. When the door opened, there stood Henry, his brows furrowed together like he didn't understand what Max was doing there.

"I'll go get my dad. He didn't tell me you were coming."

"No," Max said before Henry could turn and retreat into the house. "I came to see Valerie. Is she here?" His face felt warm, like he was blushing.

Henry dipped his head, grinning, and he opened the door wider. "Come in. I'll get her."

Max stepped into the Connors' home and cast his eyes around while he waited her Henry to fetch Valerie. He could see why she agreed to live here instead of alone in the Colony. Restoring it gave her a purpose and a way to heal from the trauma of her childhood. Valerie's focus for so long had been Henry. Now that he was okay, Max wanted to be someone to show her that her life didn't have to revolve around protecting her brother. Molly did a good enough job of that.

"I wondered whether I'd ever see you here," Valerie said, coming from the stairs.

Valerie had her hair pinned back and smudges of paint on her hands and arms, and she was gazing at Max with soft eyes, as if she thought she was imagining his presence.

"I suppose you're too busy to walk with me." Now that he was inside the house, he could hear pounding and scraping. Someone was moving furniture and laying floor tiles, and obviously Valerie had been painting. "I should've sent a note first."

Valerie smirked, her green eyes sparkling. "I have to wait for the walls to dry before I add another coat. No one will miss me for a while." She looked down at her hands and picked at the specks of paint. Some of it smudged more, and none of it came off. "Just give me a minute to wash this off."

Max watched her scurry up the stairs, heard her muffled voice and a male's he assumed belonged to Malcolm, and then heard water running. Valerie came back smiling and slipped on a pair of boots waiting by the door.

She lifted her chin to look Max in the eye. "I'm ready."

His nerves didn't calm once they stepped outside and were alone on the street. It had been easier to pledge his loyalty to Molly as The Liberator than it was to talk to Valerie. Perhaps that was because Molly had championed a movement he'd already been part of. It also could've been because he was scared that Valerie would reject him. That was a scarier thought than dying as a traitor in the old Government's eyes.

"Are you happy you moved in with Malcolm?" Max asked to break the silence.

"It's different. I haven't lived with family since I was five, and I don't remember that. I'm still getting used to it."

Max had moved out of his parents' apartment when he'd turned eighteen, though he'd joined the Guard Corps officially at sixteen. Having his parents around during that time of change had comforted him. Perhaps Malcolm could do the same for Valerie. "Change takes time to adjust to."

Valerie dipped her head. If she'd been in a Courtship with Max, he might've reached for her hand or even wrapped his arm around her. He might've risked it had they been just dating. That was saying a lot considering part of his job was ticketing those caught breaking the public affection laws. He didn't know what he and Valerie were, so he kept his hands at his sides.

Valerie sighed. "The whole City has changed in the past few months. A lot of it I wanted and worked hard for. The most difficult part is that Henry doesn't need me anymore."

"He'll always need you." While Valerie had learned to take control and fight for what she needed, Henry had learned to quash his needs and desires for the sake of others. Max couldn't imagine growing up in either scenario. His parents had always loved and supported him.

"My brother has his wife and our dad fussing over him. I try not to suffocate him, though every time he leaves, I want to beg him to stay."

They'd walked to the intersection of the street and a perpendicular one, and it was quiet. No one was driving through, so Max kept on a straight path. He knew the City's streets well, yet normally he walked them in uniform with nothing to focus on except his patrol. His conversation with Valerie was distracting enough he didn't trust himself to find their way back if they took some turns.

Valerie stopped and turned down the intersecting street, waving Max after her. "Come this way. We can talk with more privacy in the park."

Max adjusted his route to follow her, heading towards the recreational section of their district. He knew there was a park in that direction and had heard of guards being stationed there at night to ticket people trying to sneak in after curfew. He'd never had such a posting, which was lucky as they were known to be boring. People knew to steer clear of parks with guards on patrol outside them every night. Rich kids had more exciting places to break curfew.

"I know you didn't come over just to ask about my family," Valerie said. "What's this really about?"

Valerie's perceptiveness was one of her strengths, honed over years of reading people in the Colony. She saw through him, and it sent butterflies tumbling in his stomach. "I came to ask if you'd like to go out for supper with me."

Valerie gave him a smile that deepened the gold of her skin. "I'll go if I can choose the restaurant."

Max had hoped she'd agree, and he'd had been afraid she would say no. This was an easy compromise for him. "Wherever you want to go is fine. I just want to spend time with you."

Valerie glanced at him when they neared the park entrance. "It'll be my first date. Kaydon had nowhere close to romantic to take me in the Colony."

"I'm sorry you had to deal with him." Max wasn't bitter about what she and Molly had done to Kayden. Just mistreating Valerie had been cause enough in his mind, without considering how he'd betrayed them all.

"I tried for so long to stop it. He never listened to me. Not about anything."

There were tears glistening in her eyes, and she blinked them away. Max wanted to swipe them away with his thumb, to wrap her in a hug and let her cry in his arms, but they were in public and not even dating. It would be disastrous to have one of his fellow guards write him up for that. "He never deserved you, and it's not your fault how he treated you. You know that, right?"

Valerie dipped her head in a stiff nod, resolve replacing the sorrow in her eyes. "I do." She grabbed his wrist to pull him inside the park. It was a bold move, though not quite a handhold, so Max felt safe enough to get away with it.

"My dad said you and I used to play in here when we were toddlers," Valerie said. "Before Henry came along. That's why I wanted to come here."

Max would have to ask his parents about it the next time he saw them. He couldn't remember. At most he'd been three years old. "I like your sentimental side."

"It's also the place my dad proposed to my mom. Coming here makes me feel close to her."

Max couldn't remember Valerie's mom, but his parents had been her friends. He would ask them about her too. "Thank you for sharing it with me."

Valerie's smiled wide and led him to a bench. There were people in the park, whose presence went largely unnoticed by Max. He sat with Valerie and let her fingers brush his.

"I want to share things with you," she said. "We didn't know each other for very long in the Colony, but it was enough for me to like you."

Max smirked. "I'd hope so considering the public kiss we shared." He hadn't cared so much then that they'd broken the affection laws. At that moment, there'd been no Government to do anything about it, and Max had basked in the thrill of victory.

Some mischief flashed to life in Valerie's eyes as she angled her body to face his. "You don't need to worry. My dad has plenty of money to pay our way out of any trouble we get into. Besides, he would never fire you." She brought her mouth mere centimetres from his. "That's a fact that has nothing to do with me."

Max knew his job didn't depend on Valerie. Malcolm was too determined to be honourable to play favourites.

Max been on dates with Sage in the past, which had been more like meetings between friends, or what he assumed spending time with a sibling was like. Sage had never looked at him the way Valerie did, and he hadn't wanted her to. He couldn't resist anymore. He hooked her waist with his arm, scooping Valerie onto his lap. Then he brought his other arm to the back of her neck, keeping her close while she wrapped her arms around him, and her lips found his. Their first kiss had caught him off guard. He'd liked it, of course, though it had come and gone so fast he didn't get to savour it or appreciate it.

The time, he took his time, letting the softness and warmth of her lips set his alive with tingles and sparks. The world around them spun, and the blood in his veins whooshed through his body, warming him from his core. If he'd been standing, surely his knees would've buckled, sending them toppling. The bench was their steadying anchor, and Valerie was the fix he couldn't get enough of.

Valerie pulled back for air, leaving his lips cold. "You're good at this."

Max wanted more. His guard training was all that kept him from devouring her. "Not as good as you." He didn't care how many times, if any, Kaydon had kissed Valerie. She had a past, as he did. All that mattered was the smile on her face and the sparkle in her eye.

After the kiss, Max felt bold. He held onto her hand as she led him through the park to the gazebo where Malcolm had proposed to his wife. It was massive up close. Max couldn't even see over it from the park path.

Valerie started up the steps, tugging him after her. When she reached the top, she inhaled a deep breath. "Isn't the view pretty from up here?"

Max looked around. From this height, he could see the winding path through the park and the plants and flowers dotting it. "It is. Much better than the one from my apartment."

"Do you like having your own place?" Valerie's eyes went from the view to him. "I've never lived alone."

He shrugged. "I like that it's quiet, but I miss my parents' cooking. Maybe for our second date, we can go to their place. I know they'd love to see you." It was bold to assume she'd go on more than one date with him or would want to meet his parents. Max wanted to share those things with Valerie. How could he if he never asked?

"I have a better idea. We'll go there first and then to supper. Then you won't have to wait as long to introduce me."

"Perfect."

After dropping Valerie back at Malcolm's house and riding the bus home, Max wrote a note to his parents. His hand shook as he scrawled their address on the back and taped up the note. It was vital that his parents and Valerie liked each other. The relationship would have no future if all his loved ones didn't get along.

Max didn't have the luxury of a sibling like Valerie did. His parents were his entire family ever since his dad's parents had died when Max was a little kid, and his mom was an orphan who'd never known her parents. Surely his parents would be happy for him to have finally taken an interest in someone. It wasn't Sage, like his dad had hoped, and Max had never felt disapproval from his parents over that. He didn't know what he'd do if they disapproved of Valerie.

Once he posted the note, Max buried himself in work to pass the time. There were countless tasks to do while the Guard Corps was rebuilding and adding new recruits, but Max's mind was only half on work. No matter how hard he tried to let it distract him, at the end of his shift, he raced home to check his mail. On the floor inside his apartment door was a single note addressed with his dad's handwriting.

Max snatched it up, broke the seal, unfolded the paper and flipped it over to read. He jumped up in the air and ran across his living room to grab a piece of paper to write Valerie. His parents had agreed to host her, and all that was left to do was ask Valerie if she could make the time.

He thought of her that night after he deposited the note in the outgoing mail. Someday, perhaps, her presence would fill his apartment. He'd wake up seeing her before anything else, and they could eat breakfast together in the small kitchen. It wouldn't be like Malcolm's house and its excess of space. It would be theirs, not just his. As it was, Max's apartment was empty and lonely. He wanted her there to share it with him and infuse some life into the place. He'd even let her reorganize his things.

Max filled his working hours in a uniform concealing all his features. The only distinguishing piece was the nametag, which was purposefully small and difficult to read. He liked the anonymity, but at home where he was able to be himself, it felt wasted.

The wait for Valerie's response was agonizing. His next shift was a patrol, and he spent it walking the streets in the assigned section of an Apartment District. It was one of the poorer Apartment Districts, meaning it had little in the way of entertainment or shopping, and the streets were only busy with people coming and going from school and work. The shift was boring and uneventful. He only had to hand out tickets to a couple pairs of teenagers who made their flaunting of the affection laws obvious. They hated him for it, and he didn't like doing it. If they'd had some discretion, he would've let it pass. The next time he spoke to Jack, he'd provide a strong suggestion of loosening the restrictions on public affection. As it was, his hands were tied, and there were more pressing issues for Jack to fix.

Even the few bits of actual work he did weren't enough to keep his mind off what Valerie's response might be. At the exact time his shift ended, Max took the guard shuttle to the nearest uniform depot to drop his off, and he rushed home to check his mail. Guards could keep their uniforms at home, and Max usually did, but the only way to get them cleaned was to send them to a depot, and his was due. It was a delay he didn't want to deal with. Luckily there was a depot on his route home.

When he reached his apartment and found Valerie's note on his floor, he collapsed onto his knees when he read it, and clutched it tight to his chest. With her agreement on the time to meet his parents, she'd included the restaurant name she wanted to go to and the time she'd reserved. It was a task taken off his list that he hadn't requested of her. That she thought of it herself warmed his heart.

On the day of his date with Valerie, Max spent the hours before it trying to tame his curls and find a nice outfit. Most of his clothes were for comfort, not for impressing a girl. He'd never cared about one enough to do that, not before he met Valerie. He ended up tossing most of his wardrobe onto his bed before he found something that went with his best pair of shoes. The only opportunities he'd had to wear them in the past were to previous guard gatherings where the members most loyal to the government received awards and the others watched. There hadn't been any such gatherings since Malcolm had taken control of the Guard Corps. The events had always felt uncomfortable and cultlike to Max, and he didn't miss them. A date with Valerie was a better occasion for his dress shoes anyway.

By the time he was dressed, he was running late, and he scrambled out the door for the bus, hoping it wouldn't make too many stops.

Valerie answered the door when Max knocked. She was wearing a fit and flare blue dress with thick shoulder straps and a V-neck, and a pair of white shoes. She tilted her head back to look him in the eye.

Max ducked his head and shifted his weight. "I'm sorry I'm late."

Valerie waved a set of keys in one hand. "You're just on time. Dad said we can take his car. It's faster than the bus."

Max stepped to the side so she could exit the house and walk with him to the car parked in the driveway. "It's cleaner too. You look so pretty; I wouldn't want you to ruin your dress on the bus."

Valerie's eyes shined as she reached for his hand and squeezed it. "And you look very handsome."

Max wanted to kiss her, had wanted to since the last time. It took all his reserve and willpower not to ravish her in her driveway.

Valerie unlocked the car and settled herself in the driver's seat as Max took the passenger seat. He hadn't witnessed her driving in the Colony, but his van had come back in one piece.

"Have you been driving a lot?" he asked as he and Valerie fastened their seatbelts, and she adjusted the mirrors.

"A bit," she said. "Dad's teaching Henry, and I said I'd help."

"I told you he still needs you."

Valerie lifted one hand to swipe at her eyes with her thumb. "For almost as long as I can remember, I wanted my family. It feels odd to finally have them, and I wasn't sure Henry would keep tolerating us."

"Because of Molly?"

Valerie blinked to squeeze tears out of her eyes. "I thought he might get scared off, after what the Newsomes did to him. I have guilt that I couldn't help him in time to prevent that."

Max reached over and rested his hand on her thigh. He hadn't planned to make her cry on their date, and he was powerless to stop it. "What happened to him isn't your fault. You were both children."

"I know. If I have a kid, I want to be a better parent than my dad was." She shot Max a glance. "Do you think I can do that, Max?"

Max wasn't sure whether a child was in his future or not. There were a lot of ifs between that and where he currently was, but he thought he could do it with Valerie. "I know you can."

Valerie's tears were gone by the time Max directed her to his parents' apartment building and she parked along the road. It was a dusty and dirty street, so the car would likely have a coating by the time they left, which had Max apologizing.

Valerie waved off his concerns and looked up at the building. "This is where you grew up?"

It wasn't impressive to look at, just a tall, concrete apartment building with cracks in the walls and a coating of grime, the same as countless others in the Apartment Districts south of 2. Yet, it had been Max's home for eighteen years. "Yeah."

He walked inside with Valerie and headed for the stairs. Since he'd moved out, his ID card wouldn't activate the elevator. His parents no longer rented a two-bedroom apartment, deciding to save rent once he moved out. That meant they were now on a lower floor than the one he'd grown up on.

Max's guard training kept him in peak shape, so climbing the few flights to his parents' apartment was an easy task for him. Still, he kept his pace slow to match Valerie's, and she was out of breath by the time they got off the staircase.

Max gave her an encouraging smile. "It'll be easier to go down."

Valerie sucked in some shallow breaths to get her breathing under control and gave him a playful swat. "I sure hope so."

Max chuckled. "It's not far now."

His parents' apartment was a short distance down the hall, and Max only had to knock once for his mom Kelsie to throw the door open. He assumed she'd been standing on the other side, listening and waiting.

Kelsie wrapped him in a hug before ushering him inside and turning to Valerie. "I'm so glad Max brought you to see us. Come inside. Ethan's getting some drinks."

Max held his hand out for Valerie, while his mom went to help his dad. "You aren't overwhelmed, are you?"

Valerie squeezed his hand and let go as she walked into the apartment. "No. This'll be nice."

"Drinks are ready," Kelsie called as she walked from the kitchenette carrying two glasses. Ethan was right behind her, carrying two of his own.

Max led Valerie to the couch as his parents set down the drinks and sat on the kitchen chairs they'd placed opposite the coffee table.

Valerie picked up a glass and took a sip. "It's very nice to meet you, Mr. and Mrs. Alexander. Max told me you knew my parents."

Kelsie and Ethan glanced at each other, and Kelsie dipped her head. "Your mom was a caring and passionate person. She didn't have to befriend us the way she did, but I was grateful. I'm sorry you lost her so young."

Valerie grabbed Max's hand and held on tight. "It's hard to miss her when I don't remember her."

"I know," Kelsie said, giving Valerie a sympathetic smile. "My parents died when I was a baby. I didn't miss them, and they still left a hole in my life."

Max heard his father try to get his mom to a different topic, but Max's attention was on Valerie. She was leaning forward, enraptured by Kelsie. "How did you fill it?"

Kelsie took a sip from her cup and wiped her mouth with the back of her hand. "I'm not sure I ever did completely. Finding friends, and starting my own family just made it smaller."

Max didn't have a hole in his life the way his mom and Valerie did. He hadn't lost anyone that close to him, and there was still something missing. He didn't want to be alone in his apartment anymore, and the only person he could call a friend was Sage.

"My dad said Max and I knew each other when we were little," Valerie said. "I wish I could remember."

"I don't remember it either," Max said. He wished he did so he could share those memories with Valerie.

"You two were cute at that age," Ethan said. "I think we have a picture somewhere."

"Check the drawer in our dresser," Kelsie said, shooing Ethan away.

"You never told me you had pictures of us from back then," Max said.

Kent leaned forward to rest her hand on Max's leg. "I never thought you two would cross paths again. It was a surprise, and I didn't want to influence your feelings or confuse you."

Valerie laughed and reclined into the couch cushions. "We have my dad and Jack to thank for that."

When Kelsie and Max turned to look at Valerie, she lifted her shoulders in a shrug and returned their gazes with a gleam in her eye. "It's like they wanted us to meet. Charlie easily could've driven us back to the Colony."

It was an interesting theory, and Max could see how plausible it was. He'd always assumed Jack had asked him to watch Molly because he was an old friend of Ethan's, and they had a connection through the Rebel Cause. However, Malcolm and Jack were long-time friends too. Perhaps they had conspired in this. He doubted either would admit it if asked.

"You're a very smart young lady," Kelsie said. "Your mom would be proud."

Valerie blushed at the compliment as Ethan walked back in with pictures in his hand. He handed them to Max and Valerie. "We had more than I thought."

Valerie took the pictures and flipped them over, holding them so Max could see. Max recognized himself from other toddler pictures his parents had of him, but he'd never seen these. Valerie was little, with her hair in ponytails, and a big grin on her face as she looked up at Max while they stood in a patch of grass. In another, Max and Valerie were sitting in highchairs in a crowded café, and Valerie had crumbs on her cheeks.

Valerie leaned into Max's side. "We were adorable. Don't you agree,

Max?"

Max wrapped his arm around Valerie to hold her close as his parents smiled at each other, and his mom whispered something to his dad. He would've had more restraint in public, and he let it go in the privacy of his parents' apartment. It was safe to touch Valerie in that private space. "Absolutely."

When Max and Valerie left his parents' apartment, they held hands as they descended the stairs to the lobby. He didn't let go until they got outside and reached Malcolm's car.

"I like your parents," Valerie said. "Next time I'm going to ask your mom more about mine."

"There's a next time, huh?" Max asked, giving her a gentle jab with his elbow.

Valerie smirked and kept her eyes on the road as she drove north. "Possibly a bunch of next times."

"Is it my mom's stories you like or me?" Max asked as he settled against the seat.

Valerie took one hand off the wheel to brush a stray lock of hair over her shoulder. "Both."

Max smirked to himself as Valerie drove to their destination: Restaurant Doma in Apartment District 1. When she parked and unbuckled her seatbelt, she turned on her seat to face Max, making no move to get out of the car. She took a deep breath. "I know we're not my parents, but I want to share my family history with you. This is where my parents met, and where my mom worked. I've never been inside. It's not too much, is it?"

Max gazed out the windshield at the restaurant. It was an upscale place, not fancy enough to warrant a dress code or ID pass scans, just the type of place rich teenagers would go for what they considered bargain prices, especially in his parents' youth before the ration system. He turned his face back to see Valerie and the hope in her eyes. "It's perfect."

Turn the page for a sneak peek at Hosting the Peace:

book 1 in a new YA fantasy series coming soon.

Chapter 1

Kelyn patted the neck of her unicorn Saycha and stroked her white mane. Saycha walked along the cobbled path in the forest leading to the castle, carrying Kelyn on her back. Kelyn was no in rush to get home, preferring to enjoy her last moments of tranquility. Home meant final preparations for the arrival of the four foreign kingdoms' heirs, all of whom she would have to entertain. The last time Lecentia had hosted the continent's Maintenance of Peace had been five years prior. Kelyn had been too young to attend, as she had for the next four. It was now, at fifteen, just shy of sixteen, that she would attend and help host.

Kelyn sighed. "I wish we could stay out all day, Saycha," she said, earning a neigh from her faithful unicorn. "But I suppose we've taken as long as we can to return."

The castle was visible through the trees now, Kelyn and her mount having rounded the last turn of the road. She'd convinced her father, King Bekkam, to let her go on this ride. There would be few opportunities, if any, and none by herself, when the foreign parties arrived.

Kelyn dismounted Saycha in one smooth motion when they reached the stables. She liked the freedom of riding and being able to wear her leggings, tunic and boots. Her usual outfits were formal dresses and tiaras. She would hide comfortable shoes under her long skirts, but her mother would never allow it and would hear of it. Word always reached the queen when Kelyn tried to dress outside her mother's dictated style.

Kelyn handed Saycha to one of the grooms. After a typical ride, she would've brushed down her mount and fed her daffodils, but there was no time. With a pat on Saycha's back, Kelyn turned and left the stables. She entered the castle from a side door, reserved for servants, and scampered up the narrow staircase, dodging maids carrying baskets of food and laundry. Their loads were so large they couldn't get a clear look at Kelyn.

In her room, Kelyn pulled off her riding outfit, stepped into a petticoat and grabbed a dress out of her wardrobe. She would need to ring for her maid to do her hair, though she liked the look of it tied back when she rode. Her maid would also be necessary to help her into her clothes. Kelyn pulled the bell cord on her wall. To spend the few minutes it would take for her maid to appear, she untied her hair and ran her hairbrush through the strands. Her hair was indigo, the colour of the sky at twilight, and reached midway down her back. It was heavy when she wore it twisted atop her head in the style of a Lecentian princess. If she was from the northern Kingdom of Omnek, it would never fit under the thick hats rumoured to be worn by everyone. She imagined the Queen of Omnek wore her hair down for warmth.

The maid came while Kelyn finished brushing her hair. Kelyn set down the brush and turned, giving her back to the maid, and raised her arms. Her maid slid the dress over Kelyn's head, followed by a wide belt with the cord that fastened it loosened as far as it could go. When it reached her waist, Kelyn lowered her arms and her maid tugged on the cord. The belt was only meant to give shape to the loose, shapeless dresses worn in Lecentia, not to compress the wearer into a smaller size.

"Did you enjoy your ride, Your Highness?" her maid asked as she tied off the cord when the belt fit snug.

"Yes, though it was shorter than I'd have liked." Kelyn wasn't in the habit of gossiping with her maid. No servant was truly hers, and rumours would spread quickly to her parents. Gossiping was an activity reserved for her lady-in-waiting, cousin and friends.

"Can't be helped, I'm afraid, with all the preparations going on."

With her belt fastened, Kelyn lifted her wrists for her maid to attach embroidered cuffs to the ends of her sleeves. As the princess, her outfits were decorative and expensive. Only her mother, Queen Melgan, wore anything more extravagant.

"Certainly," Kelyn said.

With her cuffs on, it was time for the collar. Peasant women and those of lesser nobility didn't cover their unfinished dress necklines and sleeves with collars and cuffs. Only upper nobility partook in it. Kelyn raised her chin, keeping her head upright as her maid buttoned the collar and attached it to Kelyn's dress. It was the inconvenience as much as the price that kept poorer women from following the fashions set by the queen. They required someone's help to dress.

Over the collar went a stiff, wide necklace of bright blue gemstones. In a few minutes, she would have more woven into her hair when her maid twisted it up. Those, her tiara and the pins were what made the style so heavy. However, first came the cape, pinned to her shoulders and the back of her collar and tied in front. It made the outfit look elegant, her mother said. In reality, it hid the pins from the collar and the lacing of the belt. In Kelyn's opinion, the only bonuses to the cape were its hood to shield rain and its pockets. Today she would need neither as she would remain indoors.

With her cape on, Kelyn's maid pinned up her hair. The final touch of her outfit was cosmetics. These her maid applied lightly, only some blush, a lip tint and brown powder to her eyelids. Heavily painted faces were not the trend in Lecentia as in the neighbouring Alturra. Alturrans needed heavy makeup to compliment their excessive gems, according to Kelyn's mother. Kelyn had never met anyone from Alturra save the ambassador, and he did not adorn himself in magnitudes of cosmetics and gemstones, though his courtesans did. Kelyn would soon find out for herself whether the rumour was true for all Alturrans.

She dismissed her maid when her face was ready, and stepped from her room. She wasn't alone for long. It took all of five seconds for her lady-in-waiting to exit the room connected to hers.

Emell dipped into a curtsy, spreading the skirt of her dress wide with pinched fingers. "Your Highness."

Kelyn smirked as Emell rose. "Why so formal today?" Kelyn and Emell and grown up together and were good friends. It had only seemed natural to ask Emell to be her lady-in-waiting. There was usually more jesting and familiarity between them than formality and curtsies. Especially when no one was watching.

Emell grinned. "I've been practicing. You know as well as I that the castle will be teeming with foreign princes and princesses soon."

Kelyn laughed and set off down the hall, Emell walking beside her. "As if I could forget."

"So, how'd I do? Did it look natural?"

"Marvelous," Kelyn said. "But you must get enough practice around my parents." Kelyn herself did. She'd been curtsying to them since she could walk unassisted.

Emell tossed her head, sending her violet hair bobbing in its updo. "You forget I've only been your lady-in-waiting this past year. Before that, I hardly saw the king and queen. Never when not in a crowd."

Kelyn reached over and rested her hand on her friend's arm. "In time you'll be an expert."

Emell jutted her chin up. "Perhaps. I would love to make a good impression."

Kelyn knew the importance of making her own good impression. The last time the Lecentia had hosted the Maintenance of Peace, her governess and tutors had confined her, Emell, her cousin Lukar and the other noble children to a separate wing of the castle. She hadn't so much as glimpsed one foreign noble. This time, she would come face-to-face with them. "I'm sure we both will."

Kelyn and Emell traipsed down the staircase to the ground floor on the castle. Seeing her parents in their throne room wasn't her favourite activity, but they'd been summoned. When the king and queen summoned, one had to go.

Two guards in ornamental livery flanked the door. The one on the left bowed to Kelyn while the one on the right opened the door. Kelyn tipped her head, all the acknowledgement they were due, and strode through the doors with Lady Emell. As soon as they were clear of the threshold, the doors shut with a clang, closing Kelyn and Emell into the dark throne room lit only by glow light sconces along the walls.

Keeping her head up, Kelyn walked down the carpeted aisle with Lady

Emell. At the end, both girls dipped into curtsies. "Mother, Father," Kelyn said. "You wished to speak to us?"

"We do," her father said, his piercing gold eyes pointed at her. "Preparations for the Maintenance of Peace are going well, but I'd like to hear from you whether you feel ready. You know, Kelyn, you'll be responsible for entertaining and pleasing the heirs. They are all near your age."

"Yes, Father. I'm ready." Kelyn had spent the previous year preparing. She knew the major points about each of the heirs, though there was likely plenty she didn't know. Ambassadors could only report so much.

"Excellent. Now, Lady Emell," the king said, having finished with Kelyn. "Are you prepared for your duties?"

While Kelyn had studied how to entertain the foreign heirs, Emell had learned to cater to the nobles that would accompany them. "I am, Your Majesty."

"Now that that's settled," the queen said, interest sparking in her purple eyes. "Tell me which outfit you've selected from the welcome banquet. It is important to make a strong first impression."

Kelyn's mother did not care what Lady Emell wore. Ladies-in-waiting wouldn't eat in the dining room for the welcome banquet or any meals during the Peace until the tournament's victory feast. This question was directed at Kelyn alone. She didn't think anyone would care as much as her mother did about what she wore. "My silver dress with the pink accents." It was both neutral enough to not offend any of the foreigners and lavish enough to appease her mother.

www.ingramcontent.com/pod-product-compliance
Lightning Source LLC
Chambersburg PA
CBHW020503310726
48979CB00016B/2766/J

* 9 7 8 1 7 3 8 3 5 6 8 0 5 *